"Maggie Conner, If You Were Going For The Drop-To-My-Knees, Howling-At-The-Moon, Begging-For-A-Kiss Kind Of Look Tonight—" Nick Paused And Grinned Slowly "—You Succeeded."

Maggie broke into a wide smile, suddenly feeling as if she were walking on a cloud.

Be still my heart, she mused, then paused at that thought. Wasn't she the one trying to find him true love? The woman of his dreams? She swatted away all thoughts of making a match for this gorgeous man. She wasn't finding him anything or anyone. Not tonight, anyway.

Well, this was it. Decision time. Did she buy a ticket to Uninhibited City or stay in Safe-and-Dull Junction forever? She grabbed the champagne from the tray and was about to take a sip when Nick stopped her.

"We haven't made a toast." He raised his glass, his eyes smoky. "To a magical night."

Maggie smiled, clinked her glass with his and added, "To a magical night for everyone."

Dear Reader,

This season of harvest brings a cornucopia of six new passionate, powerful and provocative love stories from Silhouette Desire for your enjoyment.

Don't miss our current MAN OF THE MONTH title, Cindy Gerard's *Taming the Outlaw*, a reunion romance featuring a cowboy dealing with the unexpected consequences of a hometown summer of passion. And of course you'll want to read Katherine Garbera's *Cinderella's Convenient Husband*, the tenth absorbing title in Silhouette Desire's DYNASTIES: THE CONNELLYS continuity series.

A Navy SEAL is on a mission to win the love of the woman he left behind, in *The SEAL's Surprise Baby* by Amy J. Fetzer, while a TV anchorwoman gets up close and personal with a high-ranking soldier in *The Royal Treatment* by Maureen Child. This is the latest title in the exciting Silhouette crossline series CROWN AND GLORY.

Opposites attract when a sexy hunk and a matchmaker share digs in *Hearts Are Wild* by Laura Wright. And in *Secrets, Lies and...Passion* by Linda Conrad, a single mom is drawn into a web of desire and danger by the lover who jilted her at the altar years before...or did he?

Experience all six of these sensuous romances from Silhouette Desire this month, and guarantee that your Halloween will be all treat, no trick.

Enjoy!

Joan Marlow Golan

Joan Marlow Golan
Senior Editor, Silhouette Desire

Please address questions and book requests to:
Silhouette Reader Service
U.S.: 3010 Walden Ave., P.O. Box 1325, Buffalo, NY 14269
Canadian: P.O. Box 609, Fort Erie, Ont. L2A 5X3

Hearts Are Wild
LAURA WRIGHT

Published by Silhouette Books
America's Publisher of Contemporary Romance

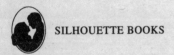 SILHOUETTE BOOKS

ISBN 0-373-76469-3

HEARTS ARE WILD

Books by Laura Wright

Silhouette Desire

Cinderella & the Playboy #1451
Hearts Are Wild #1469

LAURA WRIGHT

has spent most of her life immersed in the world of acting, singing and competitive ballroom dancing. But when she started writing romance, she knew she'd found the true desire of her heart! Although born and raised in Minneapolis, Laura has also lived in New York City, Milwaukee and Columbus, Ohio. Currently, she is happy to have set down her bags and made Los Angeles her home. And a blissful home it is—one that she shares with her theater production manager husband, Daniel, and three spoiled dogs. During those few hours of downtime from her beloved writing, Laura enjoys going to art galleries and movies, cooking for her hubby, walking in the woods, lazing around lakes, puttering in the kitchen and frolicking with her animals. Laura would love to hear from you. You can write to her at P.O. Box 5811 Sherman Oaks, CA 91413 or e-mail her at laurawright@laurawright.com.

To Julie Hogan, you're the best!

And to David Ankrum—a big thank-you, my friend.

One

Tired Of Kissing Frogs? Find Your Prince Or Princess Today, And Live Happily Ever After!

Maggie Conner drew a line through the ninth slogan idea scribbled on her yellow legal pad. It was ten-thirty in the morning and already she was sweating. June in Santa Flora was paradise, seventy-two degrees with ocean breezes to make you sigh, so obviously the heat that raced through her blood stemmed from her encroaching anxiety, not the weather.

After years of working days, weekends and holidays at an assortment of jobs, Maggie had saved enough to open her own matchmaking service. Her family's legacy would finally be recognized now that she'd hung her shingle over the sandy sidewalk that ran along the main drag of the small California sea-side community she loved so much.

Even though Maggie's Matches wasn't officially opening for another four weeks, her sign had been out for a few days and word was spreading fast. She'd already had several people sign up in advance. Sure, they were all women, she mused as she flicked an errant strand of long, dark hair back off her heart-shaped face. But the men would follow. At least, she prayed they would.

Leaning back in her chair, Maggie glanced up at the picture that hung above the front door. The photograph that would always serve as a reminder—a testament, really—that love can always be found especially if you have a determined Conner match-maker in your corner.

In the black-and-white photograph, the Santa Flora Botanical Gardens served as backdrop to three fig-ures dressed in forties garb. A man and a woman faced each other, hands held, gazes locked, mouths curved into brilliant smiles. And standing beside the happy couple was Maggie's grandma, not a day over thirty, beaming like a new mother. It had been her grandma's first "case."

Her grandma was retired from matchmaking now, but Maggie could still look at that picture and feel the woman's pride at bringing those two people to-gether.

Throughout most of her twenty-five years, Maggie had yearned to feel that pride, longed to capture that look of happiness that twinkled in her grandma's eyes. And Maggie just knew that carrying on her family's legacy would give her that happiness for the first time.

"Well, Mags," she said, glancing down at slogan number ten. "You sure won't be a success without customers."

Get A Good Girl Here! the next slogan read.

Maggie rolled her eyes. That one definitely came from the four-in-the-morning brainstorming pile.

Don't Let Your Soul Mate Slip Away! the last one read.

She snorted and dragged the pencil over the scrawled line until it was completely obscured. Everything was riding on Maggie's Matches being a hit, but she wasn't ready to resort to scare tactics.

The bell over the door jingled as she tore off the piece of paper, crumpled it up in a ball and tossed it across the room. "This is hopeless," she said, and heard the defeat thick in her own voice. "I'll never come up with the perfect slogan for this place."

"How about, Warning—Dangerous Curves Ahead. Turn Back Now?"

Maggie gasped at the unfamiliar baritone and looked up. Straight into a pair of the sexiest green eyes she'd ever seen. For a moment, she was hypnotized by the man standing before her. Her pulse racing, she stared—into the two deep, playful and highly mysterious pools of emerald—as the moments ticked anxiously by.

Swallowing hard, Maggie forced her gaze away and fought for the control she'd always prided herself on. From the day she'd discovered that the men in her family didn't stick around, she'd also learned how to keep men from affecting her.

And she'd been darned good at it, too, Maggie thought as she reached for the locket around her neck. Her pulse hadn't hopscotched about in her throat at the sight of a good-looking guy for years. But then, she hadn't met too many men with eyes like this one.

After standing and smoothing the wrinkles from her wrinkle-free pants, she met his gaze once again. "I'm sorry, sir, but I was—" She stopped midapology and blinked. Several times, in fact. Perhaps it was time to get her eyes checked, because just a second ago, with the sun pouring in behind him, she would've sworn that this man was dark, suave and sophisticated. But he wasn't. Far from it.

Sure, he was tall with a powerful, well-muscled body, as far as she could tell under all that leather and denim. But, she mused, taking in the motorcycle helmet tucked under one arm, unless the Harley-Davidson that she was certain sat parked outside happened to be named Sophistication, he was far from refined. *Rugged* was the word that best described him. A sexy, rough-and-tumble kind of man that you might see in an action-adventure movie.

Her gaze moved over his strong, angular face. His rich-brown hair was pulled into a long, loose ponytail. His hands were large and callused and he had a few days' growth of stubble on his jaw.

If this man was looking to find a love match, it wasn't going to be an easy undertaking. The women in Santa Flora were particular and liked their men well-groomed and stylish. In her conversations with them, she'd found out that her female clients were looking for long-term relationships, marriage and children. Not tearing down the Pacific Coast Highway on the back of a motorcycle with Russell Crowe's twin.

That's not to say she wouldn't try to find him a match. She was all over a challenge. And, jeez, who knew? There just might be a bad girl out there for this bad boy.

She applied her most professional smile. "Welcome to Maggie's Matches, sir."

"Thank you."

Her heart executed a perfect somersault. Deep eyes, deeper voice.

"Didn't mean to startle you when I came in," he said, his husky tone wrapping around her like flannel pajamas on a rainy night.

"It's no problem," she managed. "I was just doing some paperwork. Getting ready for my grand opening." Feeling at a disadvantage, Maggie walked around the desk and stood beside him. But being so close to him didn't make her feel the least bit in control. Instead she felt rather breathless, as if she'd just sprinted up ten flights of stairs.

Lord, he was tall. The top of her head barely cleared his shoulders. He looked like a modern-day warrior in his white T-shirt and worn leather vest, his tanned arms corded with muscle and sprinkled with hair.

If her female clients reacted to him the way Maggie was, then maybe this man's search for love wouldn't be as difficult as she'd first thought. "We're not opening for another four weeks yet, sir. But if you'd like to fill out a questionnaire, I'll put you on the list. We'll schedule a time for the video whenever it's—"

He laughed, a rich sound that filled the room. "I'm not here to get a date."

Her smile faded as she watched her first potential male client try to wriggle off the hook. "I understand. Coming to a matchmaker is a little weird at first, but if you'd—"

"Honestly," he said quickly. "I'm not looking for a match or a matchmaker. I'm Nick Kaplan."

He was looking at her as though he expected her to know that name. Know *him*. She took several mental steps back. Could he be a referral from a friend?

"Your grandmother sent me over," he said.

Maggie's brow furrowed. "My grandmother?"

A month ago Kitty Conner had packed up all her stuff and moved into a retirement village. She'd wanted to be near her friends, and even though Maggie had assured her grandmother that she didn't feel the need for privacy, Kitty had told Maggie that she was getting it, anyway. It was no secret that Kitty wanted her granddaughter to find a man. And she'd thought that moving out was a sure-fire way to get the ball rolling. To help with living expenses, her grandma had offered to find Maggie a suitable roommate. Someone closer in age and energy level. And supposedly she had. An out-of-towner. The girl was moving in this weekend.

Perhaps Mr. Harley-Davidson here was helping with the move, Maggie thought. Heck, maybe this was the roommate's brother. A shot of awareness erupted in her stomach. If that was the case, this hunk of man would be hanging around her house from time to time.

"No one was at your house," he said, breaking off her horrifyingly alluring thoughts. "So she gave me your business address."

"What can I do for you?" Good Lord. Had she drenched that query in "come-hither" cream or what?

A sparkle of amusement played in his eyes. "Well, the keys would do for a start."

Yep. Friend or boyfriend or brother. The almost desperate desire for it to be brother surprised her. "Keys. Sure." She reached over the desk, grabbed her purse and took out three small plastic bags with crisp labels on them. She took a set of keys from one.

"Are you taking her over to my house now?"

"Excuse me?"

"Is she in town yet, or is she still getting in this weekend?"

"She?"

Maggie glanced up at him, frustrated. "The woman who's renting the room in my house?"

"I don't understand. There's no—" He stopped midsentence, his brow furrowed. Then a slow smile made its way to his lips. "Let me introduce myself again," he said, amused. "I'm Nick Kaplan." He stuck out his hand. "Your new roommate."

Maggie just stood there, blank and wordless as the sounds of another Saturday at the beach floated through the open door. Her roommate? What was he talking about? He couldn't be serious. She cocked her head, narrowed her eyes. Then again, he looked pretty darn serious.

"*Mr.* Kaplan," she began slowly, her tone controlled. Very controlled. "Obviously, there's been a mistake."

He grabbed a bunch of papers from his back pocket. "There's no mistake."

"Misunderstanding, then."

"I don't think so."

She stared blindly at the pages he thrust at her. "What's that?"

He handed it to her. "A copy of the signed lease agreement."

Grasping the paper with two shaky hands, Maggie scanned the paper. "This shows my room was rented to a quiet, responsible, nonsmoking—" She gasped, stared at the box checked "male," then lowered her gaze to the chirpy signature at the bottom. Kitty Conner. No. She *didn't*. No. She *hadn't*. Maggie looked up, feeling like a balloon that had just had all the air let out of it.

"Well, I am quiet and nonsmoking." His grin widened. "And I'm definitely male."

She swallowed tightly. He was most certainly male, she thought a little bit hysterically. An incredible hunk, in fact. If you liked that type and—God help her—apparently, she did. This was horrible, not to mention incredibly embarrassing. How could her grandmother have rented a room to this man without even telling her?

Well, it didn't matter how. She'd just have to undo what her grandma had done. It was one thing to have Nick visiting his sister at the house once in a while, but living, sleeping…showering…

"I'm really sorry, Mr. Kaplan, but you can't live in my house."

He leaned back against the desk and crossed his arms over his chest, flashing her a grin. "You got a body buried in the backyard or something?"

She inhaled sharply. "Of course not."

He chuckled. "I was joking, Maggie." He shook his head. "Look, I understand you think there was some kind of error here. But if that's the case, it was you or your grandmother's mistake, not mine."

The scents of leather and salt air and sunshine emanated from him. Maggie had a most undignified desire to grab the lapels of his jacket and bury her face in his chest, breathe him in. But she didn't do things like that. She didn't even entertain thoughts like that. She thrust the papers at him. "I'm very sorry, but I can't live with a—" she looked him over from head to toe "—a guy."

"Why not?" His amused query was accompanied by a devastating grin.

Why not? Why not? She racked her muddled brain for the right answer. Preferably one that didn't make her sound as if she was on medication: I don't trust myself around a man like you; You are a direct threat to my self-imposed resolve; Hormones I didn't even know I possess are doing jumping jacks in my bloodstream since you walked in. Oh, yeah, that explanation would go over big.

She began to pace. "I don't even know you." That sounded good—and it was true, very true.

"I'm thirty years old, I own a construction firm. I love motorcycles, mutts and Louis Armstrong."

She squinted at him. "Harmless, huh?"

The devil himself couldn't have grinned any wider. "I didn't say that."

She caught the gasp before it could escape her parted lips. "Look, again, I really do apologize, but I think it's best if you find another place."

"That's not possible." All humor evaporated from his voice. "It's summer. Santa Flora's packed with tourists. No apartments, no hotels, no nothing."

"You could stay outside the city," she offered.

"No, I can't. I have to be here in town. My job starts Monday and I need to be close to the site."

She stopped and looked at him, desperation making her clutch at improbabilities. "Maybe you could find a camper? Or a large van?"

He turned and pointed to the parking lot where his motorcycle sat parked under a large oak. "That's the only transportation I own."

"How about friends?" she asked. "Family maybe?"

His jaw tightened. "No."

Her hands on her hips, she stared at him. He stared back. They were like two gunslingers waiting for the other to back down.

Her grandma's clock chimed. Eleven o'clock.

"I have clients coming," she said, her gaze locked with his.

"And I have a signed and very legal lease agreement."

Ohhh, she really despised people who stated the obvious. Her grandmother was going to hear about this. The bell over the front door rang and her "appointments" came sashaying through the door in a cloud of bleached-blond hair and siliconed curves.

With practiced professionalism and a forced smile, Maggie asked Nick to excuse her, then greeted the two women and ushered them into the video room. When she returned, Nick hadn't moved an inch. Which didn't surprise her.

"Maybe you could come back this afternoon," she began.

"Sure, no problem. If you just hand over those keys, I can get settled and meet you back here by—"

"That's not what I meant."

"Maggie, I'm not going anywhere." He dropped his helmet on her desk with a thud. "I start the most important job of my career on Monday, and I'm not going to be living out of a cardboard box while you work out your fears of cohabitation."

Soft giggles twittered from the other room. Her buxom clients were getting restless. She needed to get to work. She tipped up her chin in the universal symbol for "So, you wanna go a couple of rounds?"

Okay. If he was going to act like a jackass, she'd just treat him like one.

A half hour later, the storefront air heavy with expensive perfume, Nick wished he'd done as Maggie had asked: left and come back later. That damn stubborn streak of his had landed him in the middle of a circus—forced into service by one sexy little ringmaster.

Because Maggie's tripod hadn't arrived yet, she'd dropped the video camera on his shoulder and told him to hold it steady while she conducted the interviews with the *Baywatch* twins.

Obviously, she saw him as labor, pure and simple. No shock there. From the moment she'd pinned him with that liquid-blue gaze of hers, the assumptions about who he was and what side of the tracks he'd crossed over had read crystal clear. He was used to that look—the one that declared "I bet his brains are in his biceps."

Little did Miss Librarian know. And Maggie Conner could sure put on the librarian routine. Hell, she even dressed like one—simple, no frills—in tan pants and a blue blouse. But her bossy attitude and husky voice told an altogether different story. Not to mention her petite figure. Which was all curves.

And there was nothing Nick Kaplan liked better than riding risky curves. On his bike or off.

But this road was off-limits.

He could tell that the dark-haired beauty was one of those girls with a bookful of rules—strings, home and hearth commitments and all that. Hell, she was a professional matchmaker. He didn't mess with people who believed in love, no matter how strong the attraction. Especially not now.

Three weeks ago he'd won the bid of a lifetime—the bid that had brought him here. The bid that would catapult him into the leagues of the big boys of the contracting world. He didn't need distractions. He just needed a room.

"I like Mexican food, fruit smoothies and going to the beach," one of the *Baywatch* twins said into the video camera.

"And what kind of man are you looking for, Heather?" Maggie asked. Maggie sat on a chair just below the camera so it would look as if Heather was speaking directly into the lens.

"I'm looking for a sweet, sensitive man," Heather practically cooed. "A man who wants to come home to a good woman every night."

Nick snorted. His reluctant roommate was casting her line into a pond of sitting ducks. A pond he, himself, was never going to swim in. He enjoyed his freedom way too much. When you knew firsthand how it felt to be stifled, held back and restricted, nothing and no one was incentive enough to let your wings get clipped.

"He should be very intelligent," Heather said.

On the sidelines, the second blonde nodded her agreement. "And smart, too."

Nick coughed to cover his laughter.

Maggie glanced over her shoulder, her eyes narrowed in warning. He winked at her and she blushed, turning right back around. But the image of her was already burned in his mind. Hair pulled off her flawless face in a bun style, full, pale-pink lips and large, bright eyes in the exact shade of a Montana sky first thing in the morning.

He remembered that sky well. A few years back, he'd been traveling to Iowa for a job and he'd stopped his motorcycle on the side of the road and stared at it for a good hour. Prettiest sight he'd ever seen.

"And of course, he's got to know how to dress," Heather continued.

Nick stifled a groan. This was ridiculous. This wasn't how two people got together. Videotapes and a grocery list of attributes. Chemistry was chemistry. Man and woman. Heat and passion and sparks—there was no getting around that. And no way to tell whether you had it until you were face-to-face, not video screen to wishful thinker. But, hey, it wasn't any of his business. He just wanted those keys and a couple of good nights' rest.

"And I like to read," Heather said. "So it would be great if he could read, too."

It felt as though a week had gone by when Maggie finally thanked the *Baywatch* twins and walked them to the door.

But she wasted no time in rushing back into the video room and scolding him. "Well?" she demanded, looking like a grenade whose pin had been pulled.

"Well, what?" he asked as he removed the videotape from the camera and handed it to her. "What did I do?"

"You were laughing at my clients."

"I didn't laugh at them," he said, curbing a chuckle. "Now, can we talk keys?"

She ignored his request completely. "Oh, please. Do you really expect me to believe that coughing spasm was some preliminary sign of bronchitis?"

"Listen, sweetheart, I thought that their requirements for the perfect guy were anything *but* funny." He put the camera back in its case and zipped it up. "That woman had a list. Like she was going shopping."

"We all have things we want in another person, Mr. Kaplan. The list may be in your head, but it's still there."

"I don't have a list," he said. "Just one simple requirement."

She smiled smugly. "Oh, and what's that? That she drive a motorcycle and wear combat boots?"

"That's two things, Maggie," he retorted with a grin.

"You'll change your mind someday. Chance meetings are more difficult in today's world." She shrugged. "No one wants to be single forever."

"As far as I'm concerned, forever doesn't sound long enough."

Maggie felt weary, as if she was about to hike a hill she'd been up a thousand times. Bachelors, playboys and bad-ass bikers. They all wanted freedom. They had no idea that being loved by the right woman beat that idea all to hell. But how in the world was she going to convince a townful of guys that true love awaited them if she couldn't even convince one?

"I have a great idea," he said. "Let's discuss it at home tonight."

"Mine or yours?"

"Ours."

She sighed. "You're not going to give up on this, are you?"

"When I want something, Maggie, I'll go to great lengths to get it." He stood before her, all six feet three inches of him, the scents of leather and virility oozing from him. "But when I need something, I'll do just about anything."

She shivered at his tone, and her pulse danced a samba at the way his gaze moved over her face.

Go after what you want. It was certainly something they had in common. She wanted people to find love and would go to extraordinary lengths to help them. But Maggie needed her business to be a success and would almost sell her soul to achieve it.

As she tossed the videotape from one hand to the other, an idea began to take form in her mind. Her first two campaigns to attract men to Maggie's Matches hadn't yielded one eligible guy. So she knew free sign-ups and comped first-date expenses weren't going to have them lining up out the door. What she needed was a success story.

It was crazy, she knew. But she really did need the rent money—her store's light bill alone was Pike's-Peak steep—and it would be an unbeatable way to advertise to the male public while converting a nonbeliever. It would also give that nonbeliever what he needed most.

Excitement bubbled like soda fizz in Maggie's stomach as she imagined the slogan:

Even A Skeptic Can See The Light. Let Maggie's Matches Guide You On Your Way To Love.

She turned to Nick, a new confidence building inside her. "What if my matchmaking skills worked for you, Nick?"

His eyes narrowed. "Excuse me?"

"What if I found you the love of your life?"

He snorted. "Impossible."

Oh, she loved that word. "You're really not all that confident, are you?"

"Maggie, save it for all those lonely schmucks who want your help."

She grabbed his arm. "No one can resist the power of love, Nick."

He looked down at her hand on his arm, then at her, his eyes dark and mysterious as a forest at twilight. "I can resist anything."

Pure muscle, pure strength. And heat. She felt it beneath her touch. It was too much.

Maggie lifted her hand from his arm. "Are you willing to give your heart a little test in exchange for a six-month stay at Casa Conner?"

His brows drew together in a frown. "You lost me."

"Give me four weeks to find you the love of your life," she said as she pulled a set of keys from her pocket, "and I'll give you these."

Two

Nick felt suspended, as if he'd just taken his Harley over one of the roller-coaster hills in Colorado and was hovering a few inches off the blacktop, his gut tight as he waited to hit the ground. He stared at Maggie. "What the hell are you talking about?"

"It's simple. I'll rent you the room at my house—" she looked up at him, hopeful "—and in exchange you're going to let me find you a woman."

He leaned in closer, breathing in her soft, floral scent. "I have no trouble getting women, I promise you."

"Let me rephrase. I'm going to find you the *perfect* woman. The love of your life."

"Lady, I just want the room. No love, no perfect woman."

"I'm sorry." Maggie held up the keys, they

swayed like a pendulum between them. "But you can't have one without the other."

"I already gave your grandmother a hefty deposit."

"No problem. I can get it back to you by the end of the day if you decide not to take me up on my offer."

For one long moment Nick could only stare. Then he ground out, "You're serious, aren't you?"

She nodded. "And when I find you Miss Right, you'll become my walking advertisement. You'll tell everyone, especially the men in this town, that coming to Maggie's Matches was the best thing you ever did."

"This is blackmail."

"Yes, I guess it is. But my business needs a leg up—of the male variety. And though I hate to do it, desperate times…"

Forget about the teeth-rattling slam of Harley hitting asphalt, Nick thought. This conversation was like walking across a field of land mines. He had no clue when the next bomb was about to go off. He didn't like being blackmailed or coerced. No one pushed him into something he didn't want to do anymore.

He'd had enough of that growing up with a workaholic father who'd planned his future from the age of five. Nick hadn't stuck around to follow that empty course, and there was no way he was going to follow Maggie's.

"Just to sweeten the deal," she began encouragingly. "I'll even throw in board to go along with that room."

He rubbed his jaw, his gaze traveling her face. She was brimming with anticipation, like a little girl on Christmas morning. Adorable as hell and just as hard to resist. But, shoot, he wasn't a damn puppy in a box for her to open and show off. He wasn't looking for the love of his life. He wasn't looking to settle down and get caged.

"Listen, Maggie, I'd like to help you out, here, but I'm really not interested in getting involved."

"I understand," she said slowly.

"Good." He nodded, relief casually passing through him. "So, can we get back to talking about—" He stopped short, studying her expression. She had a look in her eyes. Pity or...or what? Oh, hell. She was obviously abandoning blackmail for a new tactic. "What is it exactly that you understand?"

"That you must be a pretty scared and lonely man."

She turned and walked out of the room, leaving him standing there, his jaw growing tighter by the second. Females. They provoked you, and you *knew* exactly what they were up to, yet you couldn't stop yourself from following them into the other room and trying to convince them how wrong they were.

"I'm not scared of a damn thing!" There it was. What a sucker.

"Then what's the problem, Nick?" She stood by the front door, her back to him, her trim silhouette outlined in the sun. "I mean, it's a perfect solution.

You get the room, and I get some free advertising.'' She glanced over her shoulder, a brow raised in challenge. ''That is, unless your bad attitude scares the ladies away.''

If he clenched his teeth any tighter they were going to crack. ''I'm not looking for Miss Right. I don't want—''

''To go out with a bunch of beautiful women?''

''I can do that on my own.'' And he did. Nick loved women. The way they looked, acted, smelled. He even liked the strange little coy fronts they put up to catch a man's interest. Above all, he respected them and made certain they enjoyed themselves when they were with him. He was always honest about what he could and couldn't offer. Freedom. No complications.

The two things that Maggie Conner sought to destroy.

But, man, he mused, his gaze moving up the length of her as she turned to face him. She sure was equipped to change a man's mind on the subject of commitment.

Exhaling heavily, he racked his brain for a solution. Maybe he *could* find some other place to stay. A shack on the beach. Or he could rent a trailer and pretend he was seventy-five and retired. No, that was no good. Too small, too cramped. There was always the unpalatable option of showing up on his father's Italian marble doorstep, listening to the sonorous tones of an overpriced door chime. Anthony Kaplan was practically itching to get ahold of Nick so he could attempt to convince him he'd changed—that the older man's accident a few years ago had caused him to realize that he suddenly wanted to be a father.

Nick narrowed his gaze at Little Miss Matchmaker. Not one of those options sounded remotely reasonable. He released a weighty breath. So, he had to go out on some dates…he wasn't about to fall in love with any of them.

"How long?" he asked.

Maggie's smile was as bright as a twelve-year-old college grad. "Four weeks. Just in time to put your glowing quote in the full-page newspaper ad announcing my grand opening."

The salty air whipped around them. Four weeks of discomfort for six months of meals and a place to drop at the end of the day. He didn't usually make quick decisions. A good, long ride on his bike was what he needed.

Nick glanced over at Maggie. She didn't look like a woman willing to give him time to mull things over. Nope. She was ready to send him out among the wolves right now.

Her eyes sparkled, and she bit her lower lip loosely, seductively and—surely—unconsciously. His body tightened in response. He was damn sure that he wasn't going to fall in love with any of Maggie's blind dates, but in that moment he knew that he'd just fallen in lust with his new roommate.

"All right, Maggie." He exhaled sharply and stuck out his hand. "You got a deal. Let's prove each other wrong."

Later that day Maggie sat at the edge of the swimming pool at the Santa Flora Retirement Village.

With her feet dangling in the cool water, she watched as her grandma's ivory swim cap surfaced and sank with the steady rhythm of the breaststroke. Maggie shook her head and smiled. At seventy-two the woman had more energy than she knew what to do with—not to mention more pluck.

The older woman's red cardigan lay in Maggie's lap, and instinctively Maggie lifted it to her nose and inhaled deeply. Lilacs. It was her grandma's favorite scent. Even the slightest trace of that fragrance took her back to her childhood. Maggie, her mother and her grandma all living together in the same house that she lived in now. Sitting side by side on the backyard's cool cement steps, laughing at the mountain of a watermelon that clung tenaciously on the vine in the garden they'd planted together. Two contented widows and one thoughtful child. They'd been the Three Musketeers. Then, when Maggie was nine years old, her mother had died. And then there had been just two.

"It goes over your shoulders, dear. Not up your nose," her grandma chided as she swam toward her.

Kitty Conner could always be counted on to make Maggie laugh. But today Maggie didn't feel much like laughing. She had a bone to pick with her grandma. Her new roommate was on his way over to her house, moving his things into his room, likely to drop off his toiletries and manly scented soap in the bathroom that they would share.

Maggie's cheeks warmed.

She closed her eyes and took a slow breath. What

was wrong with her? Her cheeks hadn't burned this way since the day before high school started when she'd slathered herself in baby oil and accidentally fallen asleep on the beach.

And it wasn't just the heat in her cheeks that had betrayed her when she'd been with Nick Kaplan. He'd grinned at her, eyes dark and intense, and every part of her had gone warm and tight. No man had ever caused such fireworks inside her. Around him, she felt on the verge of something…something unknown—something that stirred her blood.

But those first-day-of-spring flutterings didn't matter. Her goal was to find him the perfect woman. Not an imperfect, cursed, inexperienced virgin.

Resting her arms on the side of the pool, her grandma let out a contented sigh. "So, are you going to lay into me or what?"

Maggie tried to look perplexed. "Now, why would I do that?"

"Maybe because I gave you a gorgeous hunk of man for a roommate and you're afraid you won't be able to control yourself around him."

"That's ridiculous," Maggie scoffed, but inside her heart something fluttered. "Maybe it's that you lied to me and told me that that hunk of man was really a shy, sweet *girl*."

"You know, there actually was a girl, but when the boy came along…"

"You couldn't help yourself." Maggie sighed. "You're not even going to apologize for tricking me, are you?"

"For being a matchmaker, you mean? No, I don't

think so. I will always be on the lookout for you."
Kitty grinned at Maggie's frown. "Look, sweetheart,
Nick really needed the room. And he was willing to
pay a little bit extra. And with you getting your business up and running I knew you could use it." The
cunning in her eyes warmed to grandmotherly affec-
tion. "Oh, my, I can't wait to see Maggie's Matches.
I'm so proud of you. When can I come by?"

Temporarily forgetting her irritation, Maggie allowed her grandma's interest to veer the conversation
off course. "The weekdays get pretty hectic with all
the last-minute fix-ups—electrician, plumber, that
sort of thing. How about next Saturday?"

"Next weekend's no good, honey." Kitty winked
at her. "A group of us are going to Vegas."

Vegas! Her grandma didn't gamble, or at least
Maggie wasn't aware that she did. Kitty had always
said that gambling was for people who had the social
skills of a hermit and who kept the hours of a vam-
pire.

But before Maggie could inquire further about the
impromptu trip, something caught her grandma's eye
and she turned. Curious, Maggie followed her line of
vision and saw a tall, tanned and very good-looking
man with salt-and-pepper hair waving at them from
the other side of the pool. Well, not at them, she
realized quickly. The man was waving at her
grandma.

"Who's that?" Maggie asked.

Kitty turned back, her eyes bright. "Just a friend."

Maggie stared at her grandma in astonishment.
"Are you blushing, Grandma?"

"Of course not. It's just the exercise."

Maggie didn't buy it. "Is he a client?" Kitty was supposed to be retired from matchmaking, but Maggie knew from very recent and personal experience that the older woman just couldn't seem to help herself.

Kitty grinned. "You mean, am I helping him to find love?"

Maggie nodded, her own grin widening.

"I'm going to do my very best to help Ted find love, honey." She had a faraway look in her eyes.

Was her grandma actually dating? Was she in love? Happiness filled Maggie's heart as she watched Kitty walk up the steps of the pool. Happiness and concern. She couldn't stop her hand from going to her throat, touching her gold locket—her constant reminder that the Conner women were great at finding love for others. Just not for themselves.

Her grandfather had died just six months after he'd married Kitty. Maggie's mother had thought she'd found the love of her life at eighteen, but the man had taken her virginity and left her pregnant.

It was The Conner Curse.

But as Kitty watched Ted move away from the pool area and out of sight, the glow emanating from her face looked like excitement, not worry.

"Good men are hard to come by," Kitty said as she sat down next to Maggie, swept off her swim cap and ran her hands through her short, dark-gray hair. "Nick Kaplan is a good man, Maggie."

Maggie handed her a towel. "I'm sure he is."

"Helping others find love doesn't mean you shouldn't find a little for yourself."

"I don't have time to think about myself right now." She'd never told her grandma that she believed their family to be cursed. Kitty would call it rubbish and try to convince her otherwise. And Maggie didn't want to hear it. She knew what was true, and she wasn't going to tempt the Fates. "I have a business to run. A future to think about. I'm hoping that this new roommate you've found me will actually help to make it a success."

Kitty shook her head dejectedly. "That doesn't sound at all like what I had in mind. How is he going to do that?"

Maggie told her grandma about the four-week agreement with Nick. She tried to sound as professional as possible. She didn't want Kitty to even suspect how incredibly attracted she was to Nick. It wouldn't do to give the woman any room to hope that her little plan might work. And besides that, Maggie was convinced that any and all feelings for the man would subside over time like the heat of a chili pepper after an ice-cold lemonade.

"Yes, I know that scenario well," Kitty said finally. "Converting the nonbeliever. It was one of my favorite challenges." She slipped the red cotton sweater over her shoulders, then turned and gave her granddaughter a kiss on the cheek. "I think you'll be a wonderful success, Maggie. But take it from me, try and make a little time for romance. All the success in the world can't make up for the lack of it."

* * *

If there was one thing Nick Kaplan hated it was shopping malls. Miles of stores, tons of people and a food court that sent up the unmistakable stench of fake international cuisine. He slowed his bike when he entered the parking structure, pulled his motorcycle into a space and cut the engine. He still couldn't believe that he'd let Maggie talk him into this. He was the damn head of a construction company—not some teenager with a point to prove. But at least he had a place to leave his toothbrush.

And what a place. Situated high up on what the locals called the Riviera because of its similarity to the French Riviera, it overlooked everything—town, mountains and the ocean. Like most of the homes in Santa Flora it was Spanish in style, with two small balconies attached to the bedrooms. Lemon, orange and fig trees dotted the lush front lawn, while pots of flowers decorated the front stoop. Inside the small home, the mood was something he could definitely appreciate: comfort. Cozy couches, rustic oak tables and colorful rugs. Elegant and simple, just like her, he'd remembered thinking. No surprises there.

That was until he'd gone upstairs, into the bathroom.

Hanging over the shower rod like a scene from some racy foreign film were undergarments. And not white cotton briefs as he would have expected. Hell, no. These were male torture devices!

Nick had started to sweat while he'd mentally counted off each piece of lingerie: one red-satin teddy, one lacy black bra, one black-lace thong.

Conservative Maggie Conner wore a thong?

He hadn't stuck around to contemplate that erotic little fact. He'd gotten the hell out of there, jumped on his bike and driven like a madman down the highway—making a pit stop at his new construction site before heading to the Santa Flora Mall where Maggie had told him to meet her at four o'clock.

"Four o'clock, and don't be late. We have a lot to do," she'd said as though she were instructing a child.

He'd agreed but hadn't liked the sound of a mall on a Saturday and didn't even want to imagine what her plans for him were.

But he'd given his word. And he never went back on his word.

If Nick understood Maggie's personality at all, she was going to do everything in her power to prove to him that she could find him the perfect woman. Hell, she probably already had someone she thought was Miss Right all picked out and ready for him.

He cursed under his breath as he strode into the open-air mall with its endless sea of useless junk. Frowning, he shook his head. He wasn't hanging around in here for more than an hour, deal or no deal, or he might run into someone he knew or—God forbid—his family.

But he'd agreed to this ridiculous challenge. And if Maggie wanted to introduce him to some woman who worked at the Hoagie Hut, he'd have to do it.

Beside him a couple of teenage boys whistled under their breath, and Nick looked up, following their gazes. His chest tightened as the reason for his presence in this shoppers' Babylon walked toward him in a pink sundress. She'd gone home to change. He must've just missed her.

Maggie moved with grace, with just a soft sway of the hips—not too obvious. But, man, she was all female. Long, tanned legs, trim waist, full breasts, her dark hair piled high on top of her head. She still looked fairly conservative, but he knew now what she wore underneath her conservative clothes. And that made her simple, pale-pink dress sexy as hell.

Damned if she wasn't looking just a little bit like Miss Right herself.

The thought dropped into his mind with a noisy crash. Kind of like a wrecking ball, he thought as he promptly shoved it aside. He and "Matchmaking Maggie" were roommates with a business arrangement. And he didn't mix business and pleasure. Besides, she wasn't even remotely close to his kind of woman. She probably dated accountants with beige Volvos, not a man who worked with his hands and drove a Harley. She was classic, elegant—a good girl with crazy ideas. Not to mention a major pain in the—

"Hi, there," she called brightly. "Get settled in all right?"

"Fine," he said, his body stirring from looking at her too long. "Why am I here?"

"Well, good afternoon to you, too."

He arranged his face in what he hoped passed for a smile. "Afternoon. Now, why am I here in this gulch of discounted garbage?"

Her gaze roamed over him. "Before I send you

out to find that special someone, we have to do something about—'' she waved a hand at him ''—this.''

''You have a problem with the way I dress?''

She seemed to consider this.

''You're not going to turn me into one of the suits that you probably date,'' he said.

''I don't date suits.''

He raised a brow. ''Oh, really? Then what kind of man turns your crank, Maggie?'' What's good for the goose, he thought. If she got to dig into his personal life, he was just as entitled.

''No one turns my crank,'' she said in a hushed whisper. ''I don't date.''

''Come again?''

She hesitated, her gaze slipping to the floor. ''Well, what I mean is that I haven't dated in a while and I'm not planning to date anyone until my business is a success.''

A splash of ice water in the face couldn't have shocked him more. ''That could be months, maybe years.''

She nodded. ''Maybe.''

Dating was her *business*. And she was too busy? He'd heard a lot of bull in his life, enough to know when he wasn't hearing the whole truth. But he didn't think she was going to tell him anything—not here anyway, not now. Hell, they were going to be living together. He'd find out soon enough the real reason why she didn't want to date. His inexplicable curiosity about her seemed to demand it.

Without thinking, he leaned in and brushed her cheek with his thumb. He heard her gasp softly, and he felt like an idiot. He showed her the tiny eyelash he'd rescued from her cheek and said, "Make a wish," feeling like an even bigger idiot. But her skin was so soft he'd forgotten himself for a moment.

"Just one?" she asked with a shy smile.

At that moment he'd give her any little thing she wanted. But he wasn't the kind of man who showed a woman her effect on him. "Don't get greedy," he grumbled.

She laughed, then blew her eyelash off his thumb.

Desire poured through him. Not good, he thought. He needed to keep his distance or he was going to pull her close and kiss that long, graceful neck of hers. "If that wish was for me to go clothes shopping without complaint, it's not coming true."

She tilted her chin up at him. "You're being unnecessarily stubborn."

"I'm not changing. This is who I am, Maggie. Take it or leave it."

"This is not about who you are. This is just about your clothes." She smiled. "C'mon. It'll be fun."

"Fun for who?" he asked.

"For me. And it'll be my treat."

"Oh, please," he grumbled. "I own my own company. I can pay for a few pairs of jeans."

"Pants," she corrected. "Nice pants."

"I hate to point this out, but I never agreed to a wardrobe change."

"Don't make this more difficult than it has to be." She grabbed his hand and pulled him toward a men's store. "You have a roof over your head—and I have you. For four weeks. Body and soul."

He liked the way that sounded. He knew he shouldn't. But he did.

She glanced at her watch as they walked. "Then after you get clothes we'll go see Domingo."

He narrowed his eyes. "What's a Domingo?"

"Not what, who," Maggie explained. "Domingo is a hairstylist. Well, actually he's a hair genius, but—"

"Hell, no. No way. *No!*"

"Oh, c'mon."

"No."

She stopped at the store's entrance, crossed her arms over her chest. "Is this a Samson thing? Shed your locks and lose your strength?"

"First of all, I don't have locks and second, women find my hair sexy."

"It's not the hair, Nick," she said.

"What do you mean?" he asked.

Her gaze flickered from his face to the floor and back. "Well, maybe it's not the hair they find sexy. Maybe…ah…maybe it's just you."

His gut tightened as if he was taking Suicide Pass at eighty miles an hour. She wasn't supposed to be talking to him like that or looking at him like that, either. This whole day was just plain strange. He had no idea how it could get any stranger.

But it suddenly did.

Out of the corner of his eye he caught sight of a young woman. Blond, pretty, with eyes like his own.

He muttered an oath, grabbed Maggie's hand and pulled her into the men's store.

"Good decision," she said as he turned to see the

woman glance in his direction. "They have very nice things in here."

What was she doing home from college? Nick wondered, his gaze fixed on the huge plate-glass window, on the young woman and her searching eyes.

He dropped to the floor behind a rack of pants.

"What on earth are you doing down there, Nick?" Maggie asked as she peeked around the rack and looked down at him.

"Looking for the lowest prices," he muttered, pulling apart several pairs of pants to get a better view. She was still there.

Maggie stared at him, questions behind her eyes, then she began to laugh. "I had no idea you had a sense of humor, Nick," she said, hunkering down on the ground next to him. "That's going to be a big plus with the ladies."

Yeah, right. He was a regular Jim Carrey, he mused as his gaze flickered to the store's entrance. The woman was gone. Relief swept over him.

"We can get up…" His words petered out and he stayed where he was. Maggie was close, inches away, her sweet scent impaling his senses.

Under the soft lights, beside a mess of pressed pants, she smiled at him again, her eyes still glowing with laughter. At that moment he would've worn a sweater vest if she'd asked him to.

And for Nick Kaplan—a man who hadn't worn a sweater since the third grade—that realization meant he was headed for trouble.

Three

Look No Further. The Girl Of Your Dreams Could Be Right Under Your Nose.

Rock music blared throughout the fashionable salon, making it hard for Maggie to concentrate on her continuing struggles with slogan writing. She glanced around the lobby with its bottles of expensive shampoo and styling gels, wondering if anyone else felt that the music was just a bit too loud. Behind the front desk, the cherry-tinted receptionist was practically shouting into the phone, and the older woman sitting next to Maggie was ripping up a tissue and stuffing the pieces into her ears.

Oh, good. I'm not going crazy.

She'd certainly wondered at that possibility after Nick's spur-of-the-moment price check on the floor of the store. But at least in all the craziness she'd gotten him to buy three pairs of nice pants and a couple of shirts.

His playfulness had surprised her. The big, bad biker had a silly streak, and she found it immensely attractive.

Maggie glanced at the clock on the salon wall. Nick had been in with Domingo for more than an hour and a half. The two men were probably at war behind those double doors. It wouldn't be much of a shocker after the touch-me-again-and-you-die glare that Nick had sent the bald hairstylist when he'd taken one look at Nick and exclaimed, "Now, aren't you a handsome one."

Laughter bubbled in Maggie's throat. Mr. Masculinity *vs.* Mr. Clean. This project was going to be some fun.

"Miss Conner?" Domingo's assistant stood directly in front of her, but because the music was so loud, she looked as if she was mouthing the query.

Maggie nodded, not willing to shout.

"Domingo is just finishing up with your friend." The blaring rock song ended abruptly and a soft ballad took its place. "He'll be out in a minute." The girl winked. "He's really something."

Maggie stared after the girl. What in the world did that mean? He was something? Stashing her pen and pad of paper in her purse, she stood up and hustled to the front to pay.

"Mr. Kaplan already took care of it," the cherry-haired receptionist informed her.

"He did?"

"Yes, I did," came his smooth baritone from behind her. "I told you I would."

She turned sharply, then froze where she stood. Every word of "this project is going to be some fun" melted like a Popsicle on a hot day. Nick Kaplan looked like a sexy rebel out of a men's fashion magazine. He still wore his faded jeans, but he'd put on one of the white shirts they'd picked out that afternoon. He looked like a different man, yet not quite.

Her pulse pounded like a steel drum, and she wondered if everyone could hear it, even the lady with the tissue in her ears. Surely they could see her face, her eyes, as she took in the transformation of her drop-dead-gorgeous roommate.

Clean shaven, he had a stubborn, confident face that had seen sun and wind, had confronted them head-on. Like he did all challenges, she imagined. His hair had been cut short—but not too short. The chestnut waves licked the edges of his white collar, while the same maple-colored hair on his chest peeked out from the vee. And when her gaze trailed reluctantly upward, she found him staring at her, his green eyes blazing a wild streak, daring her to say something.

No doubt about it, he was still the same bad boy who had walked into her office that morning. He was just a stylized one.

"Satisfied?" he asked.

Her throat went dry as cotton. "What?"

"Well, you did this to me," he said on a chuckle. "Do I look fine, or what?"

You are about the finest looking man I've ever

seen, she wanted to say, but the Sahara had replaced the cotton in her throat and she wasn't doing much talking. She looked around her. Did Nick have any idea that every woman in the salon was staring at him, their eyes filled with longing?

And she had to go home with this Greek god.

Maggie groaned inwardly. What had she done? What in the world had made her believe that she could continue being unaffected by men when someone like Nick Kaplan walked the planet?

He cast her one of those squinty, hooded, James Dean looks. "So this is it, Maggie? No more fixing? No tattoo or scar removals planned?"

"You have a tattoo?" she asked without thinking.

"Yeah."

She couldn't help herself. "Where is it?"

He raised an amused brow at her.

Maggie could actually feel every woman in the place lean forward in their chairs, their ears pricking up to hear Nick's answer to her intimate query. And out of the corner of her eye she saw the older woman she'd sat next to earlier remove the tissue from her ears.

"We should go," she said. For some reason she didn't like all the ogling that was going on. And, interestingly enough, she really didn't want any of these women to know where his tattoo was.

She waited for Nick to give the ladies behind the counter a smile and a quick thank-you before he followed her out of the salon. Covetous stares trailed him as they walked through the mall and out the exit doors, heading for the parking lot.

Nick's motorcycle was parked on the first level of the parking garage, and they walked to it together. "So this is going to make all the difference, huh?" he asked with a chuckle as he strapped his purchases onto the back of the bike. "New clothes, new look?"

Maggie's gaze swept over him again, taking in his broad back and firm backside. She rolled her eyes heavenward. Why couldn't a different man have walked into her office this morning? One who didn't make her hands sweat and her imagination run wild.

She knew darn well that she was going to have about zero trouble finding him a woman. They were going be lined up around the block when they got a look at his videotape.

That thought should have made her insanely happy. But instead she felt oddly discontented.

"You look great, Nick," she said. "You'll be a hit." She forced a smile to her lips. "So I'll see you back at the house, then?"

He climbed onto his motorcycle, then turned those mysterious eyes on her. "Get on."

"What?"

"I'll give you a ride to your car."

Her heart raced, then leaped. She'd never been on a motorcycle in her life. Dangerous, forbidden machines with dangerous and forbidden drivers.

The longing to say yes was almost overwhelming. It wasn't the first time in her life she'd wanted to rip through her good-girl safety net and fly. Cautious living, no risks—it got tedious. But accepting his offer, even for the twenty or so feet it would take to get to her car wouldn't just be a risk, it would feel...intimate. And there was no way she could go there with Nick.

He kicked the Harley's pedal hard, and the motorcycle roared to life beneath him. For just a second she saw herself behind him, her arms around his waist, her thighs pressed against his—

Her hands balled into fists. "I'll walk," she told him. "My car's right over there."

He nodded nonchalantly, his engine purring like an enormous black cat.

As she turned and walked away, she knew that her new roommate was watching her. Watching and waiting until she was safely in her car.

She hadn't expected that, she thought as she slid her key into the lock with shaking hands. She hadn't expected him to be a gentleman, too.

"Nick, I could be going crazy, but I swear I saw you today in Santa Flora. At the mall of all places. I decided to come home for the summer. Dad said you were coming into town, but he didn't think it was until next week. If you are here, big brother, please come by the house or call. It's been way too long. I miss you. Dad and I both miss you."

Nick stabbed the button on his cell phone and tossed it on the bed that he'd be using for the next six months. It was good to hear from his little sister. Throughout his childhood, he'd gone to boarding school on the East Coast, so he didn't have many friends in Santa Flora—just family and a few acquaintances. But his sister was the best of the bunch.

Normally Anne stayed on campus in the summer,

interning at the hospital, but this summer she'd gone to Europe. She wasn't supposed to have been back until next week, but he was glad she was home. He'd missed her and hadn't wanted to avoid her at the mall today. But he was no liar, so that meant he'd have had to tell her about the deal he'd made with Maggie—the search for Miss Right. His sister knew well enough how he felt about relationships, but she'd still tried on numerous occasions to set him up with her friends from medical school. He'd always declined.

Women and setups and explanations of who Maggie was aside, Nick also didn't want to get into further discussion about his father and "the big change." It was going to take a helluva lot more than the man saying he was different for Nick to believe him. Words were just Band-Aids. They covered up a wound, nicely and easily, but they didn't make it disappear.

But if the man wanted to show, instead of just tell, would Nick even be willing to watch? Nick knew the answer was really close to yes, and that realization made him feel like a fool.

He grabbed a towel from his bag and headed for the bathroom. What he could use was a long shower. Relax under the hot spray. God, he hoped that Maggie had taken down her…those— He scrubbed a hand over his face. He just hoped she'd taken them down.

He stopped short a few feet from the bathroom door, his eyes widening and his mouth falling open. The door was slightly ajar, but it was enough to let him see inside. Need pulsated through him as he took

in the long, slender leg propped up on the edge of
the bathtub. He couldn't see who it belonged to, but
he had a pretty good guess.

The sight was really no big scandal. She was still
wearing that pale-pink dress. But the vision was just
as erotic as if she were only wearing a towel.

He watched, fascinated, as her pretty petite hands,
drenched with body lotion, caressed one long limb,
rubbing the lotion into her skin. Feet, calves, knees,
then upward. An arrow of pure heat shot straight to
his groin.

What was he thinking? Living with a woman—
and this woman in particular? She was already driving him nuts, and he'd only been here a day. What
he needed to do was get going on those dates. A
woman in his bed, that's what he needed.

And not *this* woman, he warned himself silently
as he felt the thought jab and poke at his mind.

His jaw as tight as the rest of him, he backed the
hell up and went into his room. Forget the shower
for the moment. And forget hot water. When she was
out of the bathroom and safely in her room with the
door closed, he was turning that dial to cold. Ice-
cold.

Why did pizza always smell so divine? Maggie
wondered, peeking inside the large box, her mouth
watering. Pepperoni and extra cheese, spices and thin
crust. Perfection.

She felt a stab of guilt, but quickly brushed it
away. So she'd ordered out. Big deal. Pizza was a
bargain.

Maggie needed all the help she could get making it through that tough first year with a new business, so she'd set herself up on a strict budget. Her grandma was always asking if she could help out, but Maggie was determined to make it on her own. So even though Nick's "board" wasn't in her original budget projections, she wasn't going to panic.

Besides, she hadn't exactly promised him home-cooked meals, just meals. And her grandma had always said that men thought of pizza as the fifth food group.

And, she mused, that particular food group was going to get gobbled up if Nick didn't get his butt down here. What was taking him so long? He was dressed. She knew he was. She'd knocked on his bedroom door, told him that pizza would be here in twenty minutes and listened to his agreement as she'd heard the zing of his zipper. She'd stood there for a moment, her back against the door, listening, imagining what he looked like in jeans and nothing else—all muscle and denim. He'd been dressing. And tonight he'd be undressing, slipping beneath the sheets she'd set out for him.

A very sensual thought. One of many that kept shooting through her mind at inopportune times. And, just as quickly, she'd force herself to remember that Nick was her roommate, her project, and that this was business.

This whole scenario tonight, pizza and coziness, reminded her of those adolescent Friday night slumber parties where she'd listened to her friends giggle and gossip about roguish boys like Nick Kaplan.

Back then Maggie had experienced the same budding attractions as every other girl, but wouldn't say so— not aloud, anyway. Even at thirteen she'd understood the plight of the women in her family. By then she'd already named it.

The Conner Curse.

"Did you order one for me, too?"

She glanced over her shoulder at him, walking into her medium-size kitchen, fresh from the shower, his hair wet and tousled. He wore a T-shirt and those jeans she'd heard earlier, and as he walked toward her on the pale-yellow linoleum, she saw that his feet were bare. Intimacy comes in all forms, she'd heard her grandma say many times. Now she knew what that meant.

She turned back to the cupboard and grabbed a couple of plates. "We've just got the one pizza, so you'll have to learn to share."

He took the plates from her and put them on the kitchen table. "No problem. I was always good at sharing."

"Who told you so?" she said with a playful grin.

He appeared at her side again, his spicy, soapy scent tempting her good sense. "Miss Amanda."

Miss Amanda. Sounded like a character in that book she'd accidentally bought. *Bound and Gagged.* She'd thought it was a thriller. Not an erotica book. "Someone you dated?" she asked.

He grinned at her. "Miss Amanda was my kindergarten teacher."

"Oh." Laughing softly, she thought about how new this territory was to her. She'd never had a man in her kitchen before. Except for Jerry the plumber and he didn't count. He had a potbelly, receding hairline, ten grandchildren and he always wore shoes. "Would you like something to drink? Beer? Soda?"

"A beer sounds good. Can I get you one?"

She hesitated, then realized why she was hesitating and decided she was being ridiculous. "I'd love one." She was a bit of a flyweight when it came to drinking, but what the heck. Anything to calm her nerves. "They're in the fridge."

He grabbed two bottles, opened them. "This is a great house. How long have you lived here?"

"All of my life." She set the pizza on the large oak table next to the window. "It was my grandma's house, but she gave it to me when she moved into the retirement village."

"She didn't tell me why she moved there." He sat down, a grin playing about his mouth. "Did she get a new roommate, too?"

"No." She sat down next to him. "But I think she might have a new boyfriend—her first in a long time." She caught his interested expression. "I come from a long line of matchmakers. Great at finding love for others. Horrible at finding love for ourselves. I call it The Conner Curse."

"It can't be too horrible. Your grandmother had your mother, and your mother had you." He raised a brow. "Obviously, they fell in love sometime."

Maggie stared at him. "I had no idea you were such a romantic."

Nick grabbed a piece of pizza. "What do you mean?"

"You just said that you have to be in love to have sex."

He took a swig of his beer, amusement behind his eyes. "Is that what I said?"

She nodded.

"That's not exactly what I meant." He flashed her a very devilish smile. "Love is highly overrated. Attraction, on the other hand, cannot be overstated."

Did he have to look at her like that? As though if she wanted to be swallowed up, he'd be the first to volunteer? "Well, you were right," she said, feeling an almost ridiculous need to explain her family's unlucky history with love. "They did fall in love. But my father left my mother when she told him she was pregnant. And my grandfather died in the war."

"Did that necklace belong to your mother?"

Maggie gasped softly. "Why would you ask about that?"

He glanced down to where her hand was grasping the locket. "You haven't stopped touching it since you started talking about your family."

"Oh." Maggie dropped her hand to her side. "Well, it's not a family heirloom, but it does protect me against—" She didn't know him well enough to be talking about this. "Let's just say it keeps me focused on my work and not on—"

"Men?"

"Something like that." She grabbed another slice of pizza, barely seeing a piece of pepperoni fall off onto the tabletop. "What about your family?"

"What about it?"

"Do you have any?"

"I've got a father and a sister, and I think I still have a goldfish named Pepper." The smile Nick gave her never made it to his eyes. "So, when's my first date?"

Although Maggie wanted to hear more, she wouldn't push him further. His past was none of her business, only his present and his future. "Anxious to get started?"

"The sooner we start, the sooner we finish."

Determined to be playful, she poured her beer into a glass, then turned to look at him. "Now, Mr. Kaplan. Would you say that this glass is half-empty or half-full?"

"Give it to me for one minute and it'll be completely empty."

"You have a bad attitude, did you know that?" she said.

"I thought that good girls were supposed to like bad boys." Nick picked up her lost piece of pepperoni and held it to her lips. "You gonna eat this or what?"

Maggie stared. At the pepperoni and at his hand. Her breath caught in her throat. It was like the snake with that apple. Did she dare give in to temptation?

She shook her head, and he smiled, then popped the pepperoni into his own mouth and went back to his pizza.

Maggie's appetite was gone, and a different hunger had taken its place. The feeling was so foreign it frightened her. She crossed her legs and took a deep breath. "Look, Nick, for this project to work, we need charm, not seduction."

"We?"

"*You. You* need to be charming and sensitive."
Business was what was important, and certainly the
only thing that mattered. "I'm sure you think you
know what women want, but you might be surprised."

"Oh, really?" He crossed his arms over his chest,
giving her a crooked smile. "Enlighten me."

She lifted her chin a fraction. She had no doubt
Nick Kaplan could get a woman into bed, but that
wasn't romance, that wasn't anything lasting. And
the future of her business depended largely upon him
performing all the little details that made up the elu-
sive elements of a lasting romance.

"Notice if she's uncomfortable or cold," Maggie
began. "Let her choose the movie, be interested in
her and what she wants out of life. A woman's
dreams are kept locked inside her heart, but I guarantee you, she wants to reveal them to a man who
cares."

He raised a brow. "Oh? What's locked inside your
heart, Maggie?"

She stopped and stared at him. "I'm being serious."

"So am I."

He was playing with her, she knew. But it didn't
quash the sense of yearning that filled her. She'd
dated, but never had any man been interested enough
in her to ask what was in her heart. Truth was, the
secrets of her heart seemed locked away even to her.
And she didn't dare open the door. Not to this man.

Not to anyone. "This isn't about me," she said. "This is about you and your ability to…"

Nick shot her a lazy smile. "To seduce a woman?"

"No," she said emphatically. "To win her heart."

"I do have some experience with women, Maggie."

"I'm sure you do. But finding a soul mate goes far beyond the sexual."

His eyes widened in exaggerated shock. "Really?"

"I'm just trying to teach you something," she said. "I'm not only your matchmaker. I'm your advisor, your coach." She wasn't going to let his cocky attitude dissuade her, she thought, getting up from table to grab the hot pepper flakes from the counter. Nick might know everything about women, but she wasn't taking any chances. The success of Maggie's Matches was too important. She returned to the table but didn't sit down. "Women want to be listened to, understood and complimented on the small things. They want their chair pulled out and interesting conversation during the date and on the ride home. And then there's the walk to the door and the good-night kiss. That's an important moment."

He grinned up at her with sinful intent. "Very important."

"You don't want to rush it. Take your time, move in slowly. Women don't like—"

Maggie stopped midsentence when Nick stood up beside her, gathered her in his arms and covered her mouth with his own.

Like a rag doll, she sagged against him, his lips brushing against hers. She'd been kissed several times in several different ways, but this one was slow and sensuous and knee-buckling.

"Maggie?" he whispered against her lips.

She looked up at him, confused in mind, restless between her thighs. "Yes?"

His eyes darkened as he ran his thumb across her lower lip. "It looks like you're the one that needs the lessons."

Four

─────

It took every ounce of self-control Nick had to release Maggie and act as though nothing had happened, as if he'd taught her a lesson and was completely unaffected. But that was bunk. Maggie Conner was intoxicating. She was eighty proof, and he wanted to get drunk.

Images of lips, pouty and pink, played in his mind. Her breasts pushing up against his chest, teasing him with their round softness and jutting nipples as he'd kissed her. It was as if the Fourth of July had erupted inside him. And that was saying something for a man who'd only felt what amounted to a couple of cherry bombs with any other woman.

Inches away stood the object of his erotic daydream. The tilt of her head, her arms fairly limp at her sides and the soft liquid expression in her eyes let him know that she was just as affected as he was. His matchmaker. Why couldn't she just forget about offering him a bevy of single females and offer herself to him instead?

The idea of seducing Maggie Conner made his blood heat up like the Arizona blacktop on an August day. But it was a wasted thought. Matchmaking aside, she was his roommate for the next six months, and he wasn't going to jeopardize his living situation for a few nights of amazing—

Put it away, Kaplan.

''Well, I think I've proved my point,'' he said, falling into the chair he'd occupied just a moment ago.

In seconds the liquid in her eyes turned hard, her voice unsteady. ''What point is that? That you know how to kiss?''

He reached for a slice of pizza. ''Exactly.''

''That's ridiculous. Everyone knows how to kiss.''

''You didn't seem to think so.''

''What?''

''Rules for the perfect good-night kiss by Maggie Conner? Ring a bell?''

''Oh, that.'' With a sniff, she moved past him, walked over to the screen door and stood in the path of the night breeze. ''That was…well, different.''

It sure was, he mused, watching with a dry throat as a breeze blew her hair away from her face and her sundress tight against her body. That kiss had been *too* different, and he wanted to shake that fact out of his head. But the truth was a relentless bastard. And the truth was he'd never had a good-night kiss that made his body ache so intensely.

He put down the slice of pizza. He wasn't hungry, not for cheese and sauce, anyway. Maggie had his mind walking through an ocean of desire-filled quicksand at the moment.

"Listen, Nick." She glanced over her shoulder at him. "I may have gone a little too far with the impromptu lessons in romance. Especially in the good-night-kiss department. You're right. You obviously have that covered."

He chuckled. "Thanks."

"I just want to give the women you date the perfect man, that's all. For my business. I have to make it a success."

"I'll never be the perfect man, Montana Eyes."

Her eyebrows knit together. "What did you just call me?"

If Nick could've rewound the tape of the past few seconds and erased it, he would've. How the hell had that…that silly pet name come out of his mouth? He hated pet names. He hated people that used pet names. But it was out there now and needed some kind of explanation. "Your eyes are the color of a Montana sky, that's all."

"Oh." Her tone had changed from serious to surprised. She came away from the door and sat down at the kitchen table, where the large pizza sat unattended, all but three slices fighting to stay warm. "You must see a lot of skies in your line of work."

He shrugged. "I've seen a bit of everywhere."

"Just a bit?"

"I stick around in one place long enough to get the job done. Then I'm on to the next one."

"Sounds lonely."

"It's paradise." That lie had gotten easier to say in the past twelve years, Nick mused, trying to choke down a bite of cooling pizza.

"I haven't been much of anywhere myself, but I don't really mind. I'm a homebody. I like living in my family's house in a community were I know the mailman and manager of the grocery store and my neighbor brings me chicken soup and menthol tissues when I'm sick. It's comforting."

"Sounds cautious to me," Nick said.

"What do you mean?"

"Someone that stays locked inside a town only gets to know one thing, one way of life and one kind of people. It's safe."

"What's wrong with safe?" Maggie demanded.

It's a lock box, a cage, a cramped space that won't admit free thoughts, he thought. "It's boring. No excitement, no new experiences—no heat."

She paused, her eyes downcast, her cheeks stained with pink. "I'm not looking for heat."

"Well, maybe heat's looking for you." When the words haphazardly left his lips it was as though a fire erupted inside him. What was with him tonight? Strange place, strange attraction. He just needed to give it some time to cool. The longer he was here, the more this need for "Matchmaking Maggie" would subside.

He drained his beer, then stood up and grabbed his plate. "I'm going to take a few slices to my room if you don't mind. I have plans to go over. Unless you have any more lessons?''

She shook her head emphatically. ''No.'' Her gaze flickered. ''But can we agree that what happened tonight won't happen again?''

He forced a half smile. ''No problem.''

She stood there in the middle of the paisley kitchen, fresh as rain and cool as the night breeze in her pretty sundress. For a moment she just stared at him, her eyes clouded with bewilderment as she played with the locket at the base of her throat. Then suddenly she turned away and went to the open kitchen door, mumbling a quick, ''Good night, Nick,'' over her shoulder.

'''Night, Maggie.'' He watched her walk away. Work, going over plans—all was momentarily forgotten as he contemplated the long night ahead, and the fact that being around this woman and not touching her or kissing her was possibly going to be the toughest undertaking of his life. But he'd made a promise to keep his distance in that respect. And Nick Kaplan never broke his word.

Unless, of course, she broke hers first.

''First you'll tell me a little bit about yourself,'' Maggie instructed, turning down the lights in one of Maggie's Matches small offices. ''Then tell me what you want in a woman.''

Fresh from work, Nick sat across from her with a soft spotlight on him. He looked as handsome as sin with the customary shadow dusting his jaw, his hair slightly tousled and his long, lean frame showcased in a pair of black jeans and a fitted moss-green shirt. Two of the items from the shopping spree, she was pleased to note. She hadn't known that he'd worn that to work today, only found out when he'd shown up at her storefront at their scheduled meeting time of five o'clock.

He'd left early that morning. Maggie knew because she'd heard him showering, then imagined him getting dressed as she tossed aimlessly in her bed like a sneaker in a clothes dryer. She hadn't slept much the night before, either, and when she had she'd dreamed. About him, about his mouth on hers, about his hands searching her body, finding the restless spots that continued to pulsate even after her eyes snapped open to see that he wasn't there.

It was just plain craziness but she couldn't stop thinking about him or that darn I'm-only-proving-a-point kiss. But she was going to have to, now that they were here, sitting in her office, making a video for all the lovely ladies of Santa Flora—one of whom might be his perfect match. She was not going to let her attraction for him mess up this project. And, in fact, before they'd even sat down to begin the interview, she'd made a point of saying that they both needed to relax and have fun. Nick had agreed, but still continued to act the grumpy malcontent.

"Is this really necessary, Maggie?" he asked, dragging her from fantasyland back to splash-of-cold-reality land.

"Yes, of course it is." She looked into the camera that Nick had rigged so she could sit beneath it and interview him. The camera balanced on top of several phone books, which in turn sat on top of the tallest table she had. "Remember, relax, have fun and be yourself." She smiled and mumbled, "Wait, strike that."

"Hey!" He narrowed his eyes at her, but there was a twinkle behind the daggers. "Did you just insult me?"

She pointed a finger at him. "You're quick."

"And you're trouble," he retorted.

"Thank you." Maggie grinned. "I try." Why was it that relaxing and having fun only made her want to kiss him more?

"Could you also try to find me a woman who's into complimenting her man? You're crushing my ego."

She tipped her face up. "Can't handle me, huh?"

Nick's gaze hooded, a slow, very sinful smile curved his mouth. "I could handle you just fine. I promise you."

She shivered under his gaze. Too far, Maggie, she scolded herself silently. Keep playfulness to a minimum.

Watching Nick seemed as dangerous as staring into the sun for too long. She jerked her gaze away and returned to her task of focusing the camera. But she couldn't keep herself from studying him through the lens. His mouth was hypnotic and the way his stubble bordered it was doubly so. Lord, if he only knew how he affected her. No one had ever made her breathless. Of course, she hadn't been big on flirting, bantering or attracting charming, sexy renegades before. But the few dates she'd been on and the fewer kisses she experienced led her to believe that her attraction to Nick Kaplan was genuine and highly original territory.

But it didn't matter. She needed to remember that her business was the most important thing. She was here to find Nick a soul mate, and no matter how much it bothered her, she was going to find him the perfect woman.

"Ready?" she asked him, steadying her voice and her breath.

He nodded grudgingly. "Whenever you are."

She pressed the record button on the camera, then took her seat below it—applying a mask of professionalism, she began. "Hello, Nick."

"Hello, Maggie."

"Welcome to Maggie's Matches."

"Thanks." A charming grin lifted the corners of his mouth. "It's good to be here."

Yeah, right, she thought, but she appreciated him saying it regardless. She glanced at her list of questions, then back up at him. "Let's begin with an easy one. Tell us a little bit about yourself."

"I'm thirty years old and work in the construction field. I grew up in Southern California, went to UCLA for my undergraduate degree in engineering and architecture. Then on to Brown for my Masters. Let's see," he said, looking up at the ceiling with those incredible rainforest-green eyes. "What else?" He looked back at Maggie and smiled. "In my opinion, *Cape Fear* was better the first time around. Heavy-metal music gets me going. I'm healthy and moderately happy. And to me, stars make the best ceiling and motorcycles, the best transportation.''

Maggie just stared at him. Undergraduate degree. Masters? When she'd first seen him she'd thought—well, never mind what she'd thought. She'd just assumed that he was a drifter, not a highly educated man. What other incorrect assumptions had she made? Oh, she wanted to kick herself, but instead she pushed on. ''The perfect date. How would you describe it?''

''Dinner somewhere quiet.'' His gaze found hers. ''In the lady's kitchen perhaps. Then afterward, something different, something casual. Like an arcade or an amusement park. I want to see if she has a fun side.''

Maggie's brows drew together. The lady's kitchen... Very funny.

Determined to keep her mind on the job, she ignored his oh-so-playful jibe and continued with, ''What traits do you look for in a woman?''

''Personality or appearance?'' he asked.

She shrugged. ''Either. Or both.''

''Well, she's got to make me laugh. She's got to make me think. And she's got to make my blood heat every time I look at her.''

Maggie's jaw fairly dropped. She'd never heard anything so wonderful as those three requirements. Her throat was tight, and nothing whatever came to her mind or out of her mouth. *Speak, Maggie! For heaven's sake, speak!* She swallowed hard. ''And appearance?''

He crossed his arms over his chest, a wistful expression darkening his eyes. "Every woman is beautiful in her way. A walk, a glance, the way her lips move when she speaks. But I did have this awful crush on Veronica when I was a kid."

Maggie raised a brow. "Veronica?"

"Of the *Archie* comics," he said, his gaze shifting from her mouth to her eyes. "That dark hair, those killer blue eyes. Stunning."

She cleared her throat and, with an unsteady hand, smoothed down her dark hair. He was doing this to get a rise out of her. Well, she wasn't going to let him get away with it. She'd said relax and have fun. She hadn't added "at my expense."

"Mr. Conner, tell me about the perfect kiss."

His grin deepened. "Well, I thought the one I gave you last night was pretty amazing. What do you think, Montana Eyes?"

She narrowed her eyes at him. "I'll tell you what I think," she said, standing up and pushing the stop button on the video camera. If he wasn't going to take this seriously, she was going to make him take it seriously. "I think we're going to be here until you get this perfect. What time do you have to be at work tomorrow?"

The humor behind his eyes faded as he muttered, "Spoilsport."

The Friday-evening sun flashed red and orange fire as Nick pulled up in front of the house and parked his bike. He just sat there for a moment, looking up at the window of Maggie's bedroom.

She'd successfully avoided him for almost a week

now. And maybe that was a good thing, considering how his attraction for her hadn't subsided the way he'd hoped. Every day she'd leave before he was up and when he'd get home at night, he'd find a note from her telling him dinner was in the fridge. Night after night he'd eaten his dinner in the kitchen where, not so many nights ago, he'd held Maggie in his arms. Her perfume always lingered in the air, slowly driving him over the edge.

During his long workday, he'd think about seeing her at home, maybe having dinner together. While at night he'd think about her in bed, beneath the sheets, beneath him. Did she sleep naked or did she wear one of those filmy things like the ones he'd seen hanging over the shower rod that first day? The ones he hadn't seen since.

At first, he'd wondered if she was mad at him for the kiss or for teasing her while they made his video. Nick didn't see why. He'd just been having a little fun. And he'd only given her a hard time during the first interview. The second time through, he'd been the serious and charming man she obviously wanted him to be, even omitting the Veronica reference. Though it was one hundred percent true.

Well, whatever her reasons were for avoiding him, she was succeeding. Just today she'd left a message on his cell phone to let him know that the ladies she'd selected for him had come into Maggie's Matches today to look at his video.

As if he gave a damn. He couldn't care less about those videos. He had a staggering amount of work to do and what seemed liked zillions of contracts to go over. Maggie was such a dreamer—as if he was going to fall in love with someone in just a few weeks.

Nick put his bike in the garage and headed for the house. The phone was ringing when he walked through the front door. Obviously, Maggie wasn't home or she would've picked up already, so he snatched up the receiver.

"Hello?"

"Hello." It was a woman's voice, mature and laced with humor. "Nick, is that you?"

"Yes, it is." He prayed this wasn't his first date. Going on voice alone, she had to be around sixty.

"This is Kitty Conner."

His sigh of relief was audible. "How are you, Mrs. Conner?"

"It's just Kitty, you know that, and I'm fine." She snorted. "But I hear that you might not be."

"Really?"

"I hear you're Maggie's new project."

He chuckled. "That title makes me feel so cheap."

"You're anything but, Nick Kaplan." She paused a moment before asking, "Is my granddaughter there?"

"Not at the moment. But I can leave her a message."

"Yes, you could," she said, sounding as though this was not her first choice and she was waiting for him to suggest something better.

"Is something wrong?" he asked. "I could run over to her office and see if she's—"

"Do you have any plans this weekend, Nick?"

"What?"

She took a patient breath. "Plans for this weekend? Do you have any?"

"Ah...not yet, but—"

"Good. You and Maggie need to come to Las Vegas."

He hadn't even had time to register her invitation when the front door squeaked open and seconds later Maggie walked into the kitchen. Wearing black pants and a sky-blue silk shirt buttoned to the tippity-top, she embodied the word *prim,* but he knew what went on underneath that facade, and it had his jaw tightening like a steel trap. She tossed her purse on the counter, then turned to look at him, her eyes wide and curious.

"Nick? Are you still there?" Kitty asked.

He cleared his throat. "Ah...yes, Mrs. Conner."

"Kitty," she corrected again.

"Kitty," he repeated, looking at Maggie.

"Is that my grandma?" Maggie whispered, walking toward him.

He nodded just as Kitty blurted out, "You and Maggie need to come to Las Vegas tonight."

"What's going on?" Maggie asked him, her eyes filled with concern. "Let me talk to her."

He nodded. "Kitty, Maggie's here. I'll let you talk to her."

"No, wait!"

Maggie obviously heard her grandmother's protest. She dropped the hand that had moments before been reaching for the phone.

Nick frowned. "Kitty, what's this about?"

"She won't come alone. You have to bring her here, Nick."

He looked at Maggie and asked slowly, "Could you tell me why?"

Kitty let out a soft laugh, then three simple words: "I'm getting married."

Five

***

Finding The Person Who's Right For You Can Be
A Tough Task. Just Put Yourself In Maggie's Hands
And Avoid The Calluses.

Or end up in Las Vegas, Maggie mused as she
glanced out the window of the taxicab that was on
its way to the renowned Petrofina Hotel on Las Vegas Boulevard, better known as The Strip. The Strip
beckoned tourists with a crook of its artificially lit
finger. It was a sight to behold.

Under the black sky and yellow moon stood beau-
tifully gaudy hotels with neon signs advertising two-
for-one dinners, outstanding shows of all types and
promises of million-dollar jackpots. It was a Disney-
land for adults and Maggie was totally impressed by
every glinting light.

She rolled down the cab's window and let the

warm night air flow over her skin while she took in the sounds of excited street chatter, honking taxis and the dim but ever-present sound of slot machines dinging and clanging. Maybe someone had just snagged that million-dollar jackpot, she thought with a smile.

No matter how hard she tried to suppress it, Maggie couldn't control the excitement that flowed through her veins. She'd never seen anything like this. As she'd told Nick, she'd rarely been out of Santa Flora, so she hadn't seen much of anything. But tonight she'd left her quiet seaside town and landed here where the lights and the good-natured wickedness in the air had her blood pumping double time. And to think that just hours earlier she'd pooh-poohed the whole notion of coming here.

Three hours earlier to be exact, she'd listened with stunned disbelief as Nick had explained her grandma's request—more of an undeclinable demand, actually—that they hightail it to the airport and grab the next flight to Las Vegas. Had her grandma lost it? she'd wondered. Getting married in Vegas?

Granted, the marriage itself was a wonderful surprise, and Maggie couldn't have felt happier for anyone than she did for her grandma. Shoot, happiness was a long time coming—and distinctly overdue—for Kitty Conner. But in Las Vegas? Ever since she'd heard the news, the image of an Elvis impersonator jumping out of a plane bedazzled with twinkly lights and landing on the roof of the Petrofina Hotel as

Kitty stood beside her groom had played like a movie in Maggie's head.

If she'd been asked to plan her grandma's wedding, she would've gone with something elegant and tasteful, with a string quartet and an ice sculpture. But obviously that wasn't what Kitty had in mind. She wanted glitz and flash. It was her day, and Maggie was going to honor whatever the woman wanted even if it meant dressing up like a showgirl and doing the can-can down the aisle.

Glancing to her right, Maggie caught sight of a couple dressed in medieval costume as they popped out of the top of the limousine that drove next to her. This town certainly attracted the unusual, she mused. But her grandma's shotgun wedding in Vegas had only been the first of two unusual circumstances.

"There's the hotel."

Maggie's pulse skittered.

That sexy, raspy baritone came from the other unusual circumstance. She glanced over at Nick. She had no idea what her grandma had said to him during their five-minute conversation on the phone, but Maggie hadn't been able to dissuade him from coming on this little adventure no matter how hard she'd tried. And she'd really tried. Didn't he have work to do? A motorcycle to wash? Women to date?

But, no. He'd been insistent. "I'm coming," he'd told her, his green eyes daring her to fight him. "I've been invited and I'm coming."

Try to reason with that look and that logic. She rolled her eyes. A weekend with her disarming roommate sounded like sweet torture. She'd told him she didn't want heat, but the man had the ability to heat up every part of her with just a glance or a touch.

Then there was the actual experience of that heavenly kiss that remained with her at all times, reminding her of what she couldn't have—couldn't even wish for. And now she was going to have to spend the entire weekend with him. Hopefully the rooms that her grandma had booked would be far apart. Hopefully, she thought grimly, they'd be on different floors.

Right then Nick turned and gave her that charming smile.

Or, she thought, different planets would work well, too.

"We're going to meet the happy couple at the pool at midnight," he told her as the cab pulled into the hotel's drive.

"I can't believe my grandma wouldn't even talk to me, but she tells you everything," she said.

"She said you'd just try and talk her into waiting."

"I would not have..." Oh, get real Maggie. Ice sculptures and string quartets? She sighed and fell back against the seat. "All right, maybe I would have. C'mon, at least tell me who she's marrying." Though Maggie had a fairly good idea already.

"Well, now that you're here, I guess I can let a few beans spill. It's Ted somebody-or-other."

The man that had made her grandma blush that day by the pool. Maggie felt her heart warm and a smile come to her lips as the bellman opened her door and she stepped out into the portico. The hot air warred with the air-conditioning seeping outside through the hotel's sliding doors, giving an uneven feel to the atmosphere. It was odd how the dry heat made the mood exotic, made Maggie feel like stripping off all of her clothes. Or maybe it was the town that did that.

Or him, she thought as Nick walked around the cab, looking gorgeous in faded jeans and a soft-blue shirt.

"Ready?" he asked.

Again she wondered why he was really here. It couldn't be just her grandma's request. Maybe Nick thought two nights in Vegas meant two nights he wouldn't have to go on dates with his potential soul mate in Santa Flora. Or that she'd just call the whole thing off after they got to be friends or—

She whirled around and caught him looking at her, his smile as unreadable as a sphinx.

Oh, no, she thought as she lifted her chin and marched into the lobby. She was not going to forget her goal. She had iron-clad resistance. And unless Nick had a blow torch...

"Oh, my!" Maggie came to an abrupt stop, her gaze moving over every inch of the opulent lobby. Paved in smooth, never-ending marble, the coliseum-size room was edged with thick, verdant botanical gardens. Enormous, complex murals dressed the walls, and the ceilings were a web of intricate gilded geometrics for as far as the eye could see.

"Oh, how beautiful."

"You certainly are."

Maggie's gaze snapped up to his. "What did you say?"

"I said the place certainly is beautiful." Nick grinned and motioned for her to follow him. "Let's check in. It's almost midnight."

"Sure." She barely noticed the reception desk designed to mimic a Romanesque ruin because she was reading a sign telling her about the gallery of fine art, twenty different restaurants and the world-class shopping that the hotel boasted.

"Can I help you?"

Maggie nodded at the man behind the reservation desk. "Reservation for Maggie Conner."

The man smiled and punched the name into his computer. When he looked up again, the smile was gone. "I don't see a Maggie Conner."

"Maggie," Nick whispered beside her.

"Just a minute, Nick." Maggie's brows knit together. "Try Margaret. My grandma made the reservations. She could've used my full name."

Again the man typed. This time when he looked up his eyes were apologetic. "No, I'm sorry. There's no Margaret Conner."

Nick stepped up to the counter. "Try Nick Kaplan."

Frustrated, Maggie turned to face him. "Do you really think that if my name's not there, yours will—"

"Ah, yes, here we are," the man announced, his bright smile returning. "Suite 1710. Mr. Kaplan, your room comes with a king-size bed, and the bath is equipped with a steam shower and whirlpool tub.

It also comes with our signature matching robes and slippers.''

Maggie stared at the clerk, then at Nick. "So, you have a suite with whirlpools and robes and I don't exist?"

Nick leaned back against the reception desk and gave her a sinful grin. "We could share."

She glared at him, trying to suppress the heat that rushed to her belly, pooling low and deep. "Get serious."

The desk clerk cleared his throat and slid two gold plastic keycards toward them. "The suite *is* booked for two, miss."

"That's impossible," she said. "We're not married."

The man raised a brow, and Maggie felt her cheeks burn as she realized how prudish she'd just sounded. Unmarried men and women shared hotel rooms all the time.

Kitty Conner, she mused, gritting her teeth. Forever the matchmaker. Forever and always. But Maggie was *not* a client, no matter how much her grandma wanted her to find some romance.

She turned back to the clerk. "I'll take another room. A single."

"We only have suites available," the man warned.

She grabbed her wallet. "Fine, I'll take one of those."

"Very good. They start at five hundred dollars a night."

Beside her, Nick snorted. Maggie gritted her teeth and stuffed her wallet back in her purse.

Nick glanced behind them, and Maggie followed his gaze. Although there were dozens of clerks, the Friday-night crowd was starting to back up like a traffic jam. "What's the big deal, Maggie?" Nick whispered.

The man behind the desk tactfully fiddled with his computer. In fact, he appeared so uninterested in their discussion, she almost expected him to start whistling.

"What's the big—" She inhaled deeply, then kept her voice low as she spoke. "Sharing a house is one thing, sharing a room is an entirely different matter."

He grinned. "And you think you might not be able to control yourself?"

"I can control myself just fine. It's—"

"Me?"

She tipped her chin up.

"Not gonna happen, Miss Conner, I promise you." His smile turned smug. "I shall be the perfect gentleman. Unless…"

"Unless what?"

He leaned in, his mouth close to hers. "You ask me not to be."

His breath on her face and his mouth so close made her quiver. She swallowed hard and forced a mask of indifference. "As you so eloquently put it, 'not gonna happen.'"

He moved back a step, his eyes dancing with amusement. "So if we both agree, what's the problem?"

What *was* the problem? Maggie thought. She could restrain herself—curb her attraction to Nick and focus on the reason they were here. Speaking of which... "Did my grandma tell you she had this room-sharing thing planned?"

"Your grandmother's a great lady, and she's getting married tomorrow night. She wants us to be in the hotel where the ceremony is taking place." His gaze turned serious. "Look, Maggie. I had a grandmother like yours. Let her have this weekend the way she wants it."

She bit her lip. He was right and she knew it. Her grandma's happiness was what was important. And if Kitty wanted to believe she was finding her granddaughter a bit of romance, Maggie would give her that—for the weekend, anyway. She and Nick weren't teenagers. They could control themselves.

She turned back and gave the man behind the desk one heck of a shaky smile. "We'll share the suite."

"Have you ever been a best man before?"

"This will be a first, Kitty." Nick smiled down at the pretty older woman who stood next to him in the elevator as it shot upward to their respective rooms.

It was close to one-thirty in the morning. After he and Maggie had met up with the engaged couple, they'd all shared a late-night snack and discussed wedding plans. Ted didn't have any children and, because of the last-minute nature of their plans, he'd asked Nick to be his best man. Nick had readily accepted, but he couldn't help wondering whether his own father would ask Nick to stand up with him if he were ever to get re-married. Nick hated to admit it, but the thought of seeing his father with a good woman—seeing the man happy—actually interested him these days.

"Just wait," Kitty said. "You and your friends will all get caught about the same time. Suddenly you'll find you're on a first-name basis at the tuxedo rental store." Kitty looked over at Maggie and gave her a wink.

"He has no intention of getting caught," Maggie said. "Right, Nick?"

"Well, let's just say that the bait would have to be pretty spectacular."

Ted laughed. "Amen to that. Luckily, I managed to snag both. Pretty and spectacular."

Kitty beamed. "Trust me, Nick. Just buy a tux. You never know when you'll need one."

Nick saw Maggie roll her eyes heavenward and he chuckled. He didn't have the heart to tell Kitty and Ted that he didn't believe in marriage. They were two of the nicest people he'd ever met. He was glad that he'd come, albeit a little concerned about Kitty's request to stay in the same room with Maggie.

A weekend with Maggie. Champagne, desert breezes and one bed. Would her walls come tumbling down? And more important, did he want them to? Hell, yes, he did. But he also knew what he was and was not capable of when it came to romances. And he was pretty sure his capabilities were not what Maggie would have in mind, even if she did slip up and fall into his arms.

The elevator dinged. "This is our floor," Kitty announced, her eyes dancing. "Come along, darling." She blew Nick and Maggie a kiss and walked out of the elevator arm in arm with Ted, calling back, "You two have a good night, and we'll see you in the morning."

Once they were alone, Maggie turned to him and smiled. "Thanks for coming, Nick. Even though I wanted to give her a good talking to for this cohabitation sabotage nonsense, it's made her really happy that we're here—and to see me with…"

When she didn't finish her thought, he did it for her. "A man?"

She smiled. "You'd think I was a nun the way she acts." She touched her locket, and again he wondered what the gold trinket's real significance was.

"Well, you said it yourself, you don't date much."

"I didn't say at all. I've gone on plenty of dates in the past. And I'm sure I'll go on many more when my business is up and running."

Nick's gut tightened as the elevator came to a stop at their floor. For some strange and incredibly annoying reason, he didn't like to think of her out with another guy. Where on earth was she going to find someone who was right for her? A man who wouldn't take any of her grief, a man who was willing to stop her silly romantic notions by kissing her until she was breathless.

Good luck, he thought, she was going to have a hard time finding a saint like that.

"Your grandmother and Ted seem really happy," he said as they walked down the hallway.

"They do, don't they?" Maggie smiled. "I like Ted. What did you think of him?"

He slid the electronic key in the door. "Good guy.

We're going to try on tuxes tomorrow, so I'll find out for sure.''

She grinned. ''I expect you to report back if there's anything amiss.''

''If he has another wife hidden away or a harem locked up in his basement, you'll be the first to know,'' he said, holding the door open for her.

They were both laughing as they opened the door, but once they were inside, the laughter came to an abrupt halt. They stood side by side in the marble foyer of the suite, staring at the luxury sprawled out in front of them. To Nick, it wasn't the lavishness of the room that had him staring; it was the pure sensuality of it. Rich colors and soft, plush fabrics. Candles, roses in vases, wine chilling, strawberries dipped in chocolate.

That Kitty was something else.

Nick followed Maggie down the steps and into the living room, trying to look at the place through a contractor's eye instead of a lover's. The layout was perfect. There was a separate living room with a couch, a desk, two comfy chairs and a balcony facing the man-made lake and fountain.

Leaving Maggie in the living room, he walked into the master bedroom. Perfectly centered in the room was a massive king-size bed. Moonlight from the second balcony cast cloud-like shadows over most of the space. As promised, the master bath was a lover's retreat, filled with plush red towels, sunken marble tub and a glass shower built for two.

Trying to push away images of Maggie lightly wrapped in one of those short red towels, Nick closed the bathroom door and walked back to her. She stood in the center of the living room, staring up at the ornate ceiling painted with naked cherubs frolicking through mystical gardens.

"I'll take the living room," he said.

She tore her eyes from the lofty mural. "Are you sure?"

Hell, no, I'm not sure. "Is that an invitation?"

Her ten-second hesitation felt like an hour. "No," she said finally, a hitch in her voice. "I just meant that I could stay in here and you could have the master bedroom. I don't need a king-size bed. I don't take up that much space. It's really made for two people. So if you—"

"You're rambling, Maggie," he said with a chuckle.

She laughed, too, then stepped back to sit in one of the big, overstuffed leather chairs. Her heel caught on the edge of the thick, tawny-colored rug and she pitched sideways.

Nick lunged forward, catching her and pulling her up. Holding her against him, he looked into her eyes to see if she was all right. He saw embarrassment, but nothing worse.

"You okay?" he asked.

She stared up at him, her eyes liquid and dark blue, and nodded with the barest movement of her head.

Nick knew it was time to let go of her. But he didn't move. She felt too good against him, the floral scent of her drugging his senses.

Her gaze still locked with his, she ran her tongue over her lower lip.

"Not fair, Maggie." He groaned the words like a man being forced to divulge more than his name, rank and serial number.

He released her. This wasn't going well. He needed to get out of here, away from her for a while. Just being around her was making his head hurt and his body ache.

"I'm going to go down to the casino, play a few hands of blackjack," he said.

She nodded again, her cheeks flushed.

"I'll try not to wake you up when I come in." And I'll try to fight the urge to climb in bed with you when I do, he thought, stuffing one of the gold keys in his pocket and walking out the door.

Weddings in Las Vegas were as commonplace as bad home permanents. But women like her grandma were not, Maggie noted. By the time she was through with her breakfast the following morning, Kitty had invited practically the entire hotel—staff included— to her evening wedding by the pool. Rumor had it that Ted had paid a pretty penny for the spot, but if he was worried about finances he certainly didn't show it. He and Kitty had also hired a dance band and recruited the head chef and pastry chef from the hotel's best restaurant to cater the event. They'd purchased the fanciest of wedding finery for themselves and had insisted that Maggie and Nick have the same. So by ten-thirty Ted had taken Nick away and Kitty had whisked Maggie into one of the top designer shops in the hotel, where she was trying to convince her granddaughter that a red, strapless sheath would be perfect for the maid of honor.

"Am I being a pain in the butt?" Maggie asked after their twenty-minute tug-of-war slowed.

"Yes."

"But you're the bride. You're the one who should stand out. In red, I'll—"

"You'll be beautiful. And I want you to look beautiful." Her gaze dipped to Maggie's locket. "Don't you get tired of being the perfect granddaughter, Maggie?"

"What do you mean?"

"Don't you ever just want to cut loose? Be carefree. Maybe get a little wild?" She grinned. "I recommend it highly."

Maggie's brows furrowed. "Grandma, please don't tell me that you're trying to get me to be a bad girl."

"Just for the weekend, honey. Then if you don't like it, you can return to the safety of being a good girl."

It was the second time in two days that she'd heard her life being referred to as "safe." Once by her grandma and once by the man Maggie had wanted to fling herself on when he'd crept back to their room late last night. "What's so wrong with being responsible and practical?"

"Nothing, unless your purpose becomes giving others a good time but never yourself." She kissed Maggie on the cheek. "You deserve to have a few days and nights of decadent fun." Then she handed her the red dress. "I've got to run to the salon. You decide about the dress. And,'' she said with a parting wink, ''the night of decadence.''

In the full-length mirror, Maggie watched her grandma go. She didn't want to be cautious and boring—she wasn't boring. Whether anyone believed it or not, she did have a few carefree oats left in her.

Two women her age came scampering out of a dressing room wearing the fun, clingy, sexy kind of dress she held in her hands. They spun around in front of the mirror, their faces excited and eager.

Oh, just the thought of blowing Nick Kaplan away with a sexy dress, a fabulous new hairstyle and a devil-may-care attitude made the fun-fairies that had been waiting patiently within her for years fly about.

Maybe he'd even kiss her again, she thought. What harm would there be in a few kisses? Maggie Conner—bad girl, carefree girl. She smiled at the thought and signaled the salesgirl that she'd made her decision.

Tonight would belong to the woman Maggie was determined to set free. But in the back of her mind she knew that, come Sunday, she would have to return to the safety and protection of her life in Santa Flora.

It had been close to five-thirty by the time Maggie had returned to the suite. Nick hadn't been there, only a note from him telling her that he was hanging out with the nervous groom and she had the place to herself to get ready—that he'd meet her down by the pool at seven.

And it was almost that now, Maggie mused, glancing over at the clock. Five minutes to seven. After checking her makeup and slipping on her dress, she looked in the full-length mirror once more and let out a very girlish, very nervous laugh.

She understood those women in the dress shop now.

Except for her gold locket, Maggie didn't look anything like herself. The red strapless dress hit just below the knee and showed off every curve. The matching strappy sandals displayed her pretty painted toes and were three inches high at least, making her legs look miles long. The woman at the salon had given Maggie a seductive up-do that allowed several errant wisps to frame her face.

She couldn't wait for Nick to see her, she thought as she left the room and made her way downstairs.

The setup for the ceremony and reception was breathtakingly beautiful—complete with an ice sculpture, Maggie was pleased to note. Several guests had arrived and were milling about, talking. She wondered who they all were, and if even half of them had met Kitty and Ted.

She turned back toward the stairs looking for the bride and groom. But she didn't see either of them. What she did see caused a sharp intake of breath and a dry throat as she caught sight of Nick. Granted, men in tuxes were always handsome. But none, *none,* compared to Nick Kaplan. He stood at the top of the stairs, one hand in his pants pocket, looking off-the-chart gorgeous. Dressed in a traditional tuxedo, his eyes flashed pure green deviltry. What had ever made her think that this man wasn't sophisticated?

She glanced around. It was worse than the salon in the mall. There were far more women here, and they were all staring at him as he walked down the steps, a confident smile playing about his lips.

Then he saw her.

At first his gaze raked over her slowly, from her red toes to her red lipstick. When his gaze finally came to rest on hers, all amusement had vanished from his expression. He strode toward her, something primitive, almost possessive burning behind his eyes. The intensity of it made Maggie feel as if she was about to become his hapless prey.

"Maggie Conner," he said when he stood in front of her. "If you were going for the drop-to-my-knees, howling-at-the-moon, begging-for-a-kiss kind of look tonight," he paused and grinned slowly, "you succeeded."

She broke into a wide smile, suddenly feeling as if she was walking on a cloud. "Thank you." He looked even better up close, if that were possible. Broad shoulders, just a hint of shadow on his jaw.

Be still my heart, she mused, glancing over at the bar. The two female bartenders were gaping at Nick, trying to catch his eye. Of all the rude— She paused at that thought. Wasn't she the one trying to find him true love? The woman of his dreams?

She swatted away all thoughts of making a match for this gorgeous man. She wasn't finding him anything or anyone. Not tonight, anyway.

"Can I get you something to drink?" Nick asked her as a waiter passed by with a silver tray full of glasses of champagne.

Champagne was a fast train ride to Uninhibited City. Maggie had heard several people say that the bubbly potion made your knees weak and your senses explode. Well, this was it. Decision time. Did she buy a ticket or stay in Safe-and-Dull Junction forever?

She grabbed the champagne from the tray and was about to take a sip when Nick stopped her.

"We haven't made a toast." He raised his glass, his eyes smoky. "To a magical night for Kitty and Ted."

She smiled, clinked her glass with his and added, "To a magical night for everyone."

Six

She was a different woman tonight, Nick mused, watching Maggie across the long candlelit table as she talked to her new grandfather and sipped champagne. They were far enough away that Nick couldn't hear what they were saying, but every few minutes Maggie would break out into a cheery laugh that filled the night air with warmth. She was carefree and looked relaxed under the gauzy white tent that housed the bride, groom, Maggie, Nick and about thirty-six strangers who were fast becoming friends.

She also looked unbelievably stunning in her red dress and heels. It had been one thing to imagine what she wore underneath her neatly pressed pants and high-collared blouses but tonight her sensuality lay bare for all to see and admire.

And they did.

Men from eighteen to eighty watched, their gazes following her wherever she went. But she hadn't seemed to notice. Her attention had been focused on the last-minute preparations and her grandma's bouquet.

The ceremony itself had gone off effortlessly. And even though Nick didn't believe in marriage for himself, he was happy for the couple. Under the fading eyes of a red sunset, Kitty and Ted had pronounced their love and commitment, then given each other a ravenous kiss before the official had pronounced them husband and wife. It was all fine and very sweet and just as a wedding should be. But during that kiss, Maggie had looked over at him, her eyes filled with unshed tears, and it had done something to him. He didn't know why—maybe didn't even want to know why—but that look had gripped his heart like a damn vise. And had rendered him mute ever since.

During the toast, dinner—even while the cake had been served—he'd kept to himself. And it hadn't been easy. He'd wanted to talk to her, look into those eyes and tell her just what he thought of that dress. Every so often she'd turn to look at him, the warm desert breeze picking up wisps of dark hair and blowing them about her face. Her eyes shone like the crystal glass she held, then turned dark and seductive as she tipped that glass and sipped her champagne.

Beside him, he heard a soft laugh as Kitty sat down at the vacant seat next to him. "Are you staring at my granddaughter?"

"Admiring," he corrected.

"Ah." Her tone was filled with understanding.

"She's beautiful, isn't she? Someday she'll make a beautiful bride."

His chest tightened as he turned to look at Maggie. A vision of her dressed in white flashed into his mind and at the same time annoyance flowed through his blood. Why was marriage the goal of every parent, every grandparent, every woman?

Kitty studied him. "I'm not talking about you, Nick, if that's what you're thinking. All that jabber about tuxes last night was just a little joke. And the living together, well, that was a hope. I know how different the two of you are. Maggie appreciates commitment, and you appreciate freedom."

Damn right he did. He drained the remainder of the champagne in his glass, glad that the subject was cleared up. But then he paused and looked back at Kitty. "So this weekend was about…"

"Fun. Just plain fun. For both of you." Kitty eyed her granddaughter. "But I'm always thinking about her future. Keeping my eye out for Mr. Right."

Mr. Right. Nick snorted. "Well, I hope he's out there."

"I know he is," she said, sounding absolutely convinced. "Maybe you can help me to find him."

His jaw tightened. "I don't see how."

"In your business you must know many eligible young men." She smiled. "Maggie's your matchmaker. You could be hers."

"I don't think so, Kitty," he said.

She shrugged nonchalantly. "It was just a thought."

The thought of seeing his new roommate with another man kissing her, touching her, made Nick want to put his fist through the table.

He wanted out of this conversation and he wanted thoughts of Maggie with other guys out of his mind.

To the right of the pool, the band had finished setting up. They announced themselves and began to play a bluesy midtempo tune with lots of bass.

"Dancing," Kitty said, a smile in her voice. "The true passage to seduction."

Nick nodded, then found out quickly how right she was as, one after the other, men turned to stare at Maggie, their eyes fixated on her as if she was a fine bottle of merlot they were desperate to uncork.

Kitty saw them, too, and remarked, "Looks like I won't be needing much help after all."

Nick's muscles tensed. When he and Maggie got back to Santa Flora, the dating and matchmaking would return to both their lives. Then she could find her Mr. Right. Next week or next year for all he cared. Tonight she was with him.

He stood, walked the length of the table and offered his hand to Maggie. "Dance with me?" he asked, trying to keep the possessive tone out of his voice.

Maggie felt her heart leap and fall as she stared up into Nick's emerald gaze. This was it. The crossroads. If she was going to follow through on her decision to loosen the strings that bound her, she would just have to give in to the longing inside her.

She put her cool hand in Nick's warm one and smiled. "I'd love to."

They walked toward the dance floor, past the

swimming pool that glittered like blue glass under the electric lights. Couples were already converging onto the small black-tiled floor, which was wreathed by flowers wrapped loosely in twinkling lights. Maggie breathed in the rich scent of the blooms as Nick led her out into the midst of the flowers and lights and pulled her into his arms. It felt good to be held, and held by him.

She looked up at him as they swayed to the music. "I have to tell you something."

He raised a brow at her while his arm tightened around her waist. "Well, confession is good for the soul. Or so I've heard."

"I've heard the same thing. So here goes." She smiled a little shyly. "You are a dashing best man, Mr. Kaplan."

He grinned. "That is a pretty shocking confession. But I'll go you one better." Suddenly he released her, twirled her around, then caught her close. "You are the most beautiful maid of honor I've ever seen."

She laughed at his playfulness but shook her head at his flattery. "I'm not beautiful. Cute, maybe, but not beautiful."

He leaned toward her and whispered in her ear, "I say that you are."

Breathing was impossible at that moment. Thinking, too. He was so close his chest pressed against her breasts, his hips tight against her belly. And that scent that emanated from him. Spicy and so intoxicatingly male. She lowered her gaze but found her voice. "I forgot that you're such an expert on women."

"I never said that." He put a finger under her chin and lifted her gaze to his. "I just said I knew how to kiss a woman."

Emboldened by the smooth, seductive tonic known as champagne, she whispered, "But do you know how to kiss a woman while you're *dancing?*" Oh-oh, she thought, you're in the deep end now.

An eyebrow shot up over his left eye. "You want to find out?" His tone was low and raspy and over-flowing with promises.

Heat flooded her cheeks, and she knew the old Maggie, the Maggie of this morning, would pull away at such an invitation—pretend she didn't know what he meant. But that wouldn't be fulfilling the promise she'd made to herself today. And she was going to follow through no matter how unfamiliar—or how good—it felt.

She ran her tongue over her lower lip. "I wouldn't have asked the question if I didn't, Nick."

His eyes darkened as the red-hot sound of the sax-ophone was carried to them by a gust of desert wind. "Don't say my name like that again," he warned, "or I will kiss you—here, dancing in front of every-one. No more playing around."

She lowered her lashes and threw down another card. "I'm not playing…*Nick.*"

She barely got his name out before he covered her mouth with his. The kiss was hard, passion-filled and quick. He pulled away just as abruptly as he'd come.

"I can't breathe," she said, pressing against him, but the breathlessness wasn't from desire alone. Their first kiss on the night he'd moved in had been like a knock on Snow White's glass coffin, but this kiss had awakened Maggie from a long and very unfulfilling sleep. And for the first time in her life she truly understood what she'd been missing. What she'd allowed herself to go without.

"Why did you do that?" he practically growled as the band ended the song with a flourish of percussion. "Why did you bait me? I warned you..."

She nodded and strove for lightness. No way was she telling him that she wanted him...wanted him to seduce her. "It was research. I had to make sure you could do two things at once."

"Do you need any further demonstrations on that point?" he asked, his voice heavy with irritation.

Her brow knit together. "What's wrong?"

"Nothing," he said, then suddenly turned and led her off the dance floor.

"We're done dancing?" she asked, dragging her feet as she followed him back up to the head table. No, she thought, I need more. I'm dying of thirst here and he's holding the darn canteen! "C'mon, Nick, how about one more dance?" she asked, hopeful.

"Don't you think you should save something for those other guys waiting to dance with you?"

Where the devil had that come from? she thought as she watched his dark smile fade like foul weather setting in. He turned toward the bar, and she followed his gaze. A trio of men stared openly at her with appreciative eyes.

"Who knows, Maggie," Nick continued dryly, grabbing a glass of champagne from the table. "Maybe one of those guys is *your* soul mate. Maybe

The Silhouette Reader Service™ — Here's how it works:

If offer card is missing write to: Silhouette Reader Service, 3010 Walden Ave., P.O. Box 1867, Buffalo NY 14240-1867

NO POSTAGE
NECESSARY
IF MAILED
IN THE
UNITED STATES

BUSINESS REPLY MAIL
FIRST-CLASS MAIL   PERMIT NO. 717-003   BUFFALO, NY

POSTAGE WILL BE PAID BY ADDRESSEE

SILHOUETTE READER SERVICE
3010 WALDEN AVE
PO BOX 1867
BUFFALO NY 14240-9952

GET FREE BOOKS and a FREE GIFT WHEN YOU PLAY THE...

SLOT MACHINE GAME!

Just scratch off the silver box with a coin. Then check below to see the gifts you get!

YES! I have scratched off the silver box. Please send me the 2 free Silhouette Desire® books and gift for which I qualify. I understand I am under no obligation to purchase any books, as explained on the back of this card.

326 SDL DQLN

225 SDL DRNK
(S-D-10/02)

FIRST NAME	LAST NAME

ADDRESS

APT.#	CITY

STATE / PROV.	ZIP/POSTAL CODE

7	7	7	**Worth TWO FREE BOOKS plus a BONUS Mystery Gift!**
🍒	🍒	🍒	**Worth TWO FREE BOOKS!**
♣	♣	♣	**Worth ONE FREE BOOK!**
🔔	🔔	🍒	**TRY AGAIN!**

Visit us online at www.eHarlequin.com

Offer limited to one per household and not valid to current Silhouette Desire® subscribers. All orders subject to approval.

© 2000 HARLEQUIN ENTERPRISES LTD. ® and TM are trademarks owned by Harlequin Books S.A. used under license.

DETACH AND MAIL CARD TODAY!

one of them actually believes in that bunk you sell. If I were you,'' he said with cold formality, ''I'd go check it out.''

''Would you?'' she retorted, lips tight.

He nodded, his jaw twitching.

''Well, you have at it then,'' she said, her tone ripe with her own irritation. ''I've had enough. I'm going to bed.''

Maggie didn't have to guess why he was being such a jerk, pushing her into dancing with other men. Her put-on boldness had led her to make a complete fool of herself. Nick couldn't have made it clearer that he wasn't interested in what she was so shamelessly offering.

That room-service menu had better have ice cream and lots of it, she thought as she turned away from Nick's glowering face. Then, after she kissed her grandma and Ted good-night, she headed for the elevator.

Nick watched her go, holding back a curse. Women. They had no idea what they wanted. Acting cool one minute and coy the next. Again he'd been goaded into kissing her, and again his body had jolted awake like a three-alarm fire. Maybe he was going through some kind of midlife crisis at thirty. That would explain these strange…feelings he hadn't been able to shake over the past week. It wasn't lust—he knew what that felt like all too well. It could just be irritation or pure annoyance. He was certainly feeling that.

What he really needed, he thought, as he shot to

his feet, was to get out of this world of wedding bliss. It was starting to warp his mind. Maybe he'd go to the casino or head straight for the bar the way he had last night. Whatever he did, he wanted out of here. He gave Kitty a kiss on the cheek, shook Ted's hand and took off for the lobby.

But he didn't go to the bar or to the gaming tables. Instead he followed the trail of a warm, intoxicating fragrance. Like an idiot, he went after Maggie.

He caught up with her at the elevators. "Maggie, hold on a minute."

"What are you doing here?" she said, stabbing repeatedly at the up button that was already lit.

"Looking for you."

"Why?"

The elevator doors slid open and Nick expelled an aggravated breath. "I don't know."

She didn't say anything, just stalked into the empty elevator. He followed her. "Dammit, Maggie." Taking her hand, he turned her to face him. "Look, I didn't want you to leave the party."

She wrenched her hand free, leaned past him and pushed the button for the seventeenth floor. "No. You wanted me to dance with those other men." The door closed and they were alone. "Why didn't you just tell me you weren't interested in—"

"Dammit, Maggie," he repeated, hauled her against him, kissed her hard, then pressed her back against the elevator wall. "I *am* interested in you. That's the problem."

Breath held, she stared at him, her eyes wide and

searching his for answers that he didn't want to give, but somehow had to find a way to communicate.

"You deserve a guy who believes in love. Someone who wants what you want, thinks the same way you do." He leaned toward her and slowly brushed his thumb over her lips. "You pissed me off back there. That kiss—that incredible kiss—I don't know how to stop myself from doing that again or wanting more. You're the expert, Maggie. Tell me how to stop myself from wanting you."

Finally she released the breath she was holding. "Oh, Nick," she whispered, wrapping her arms around his neck. "I'm no expert. I don't even know how to stop wanting you."

On a desperate groan, he covered her mouth again, kissing her deeply. "Why do you feel so good?"

She whimpered her response, her mouth slanting, taking his tongue into her slick warmth. His groin tightened, lust ripping into him, longing filling every empty corner inside him. She tasted like champagne. Sweet as hell. He wanted to taste every inch of her. With each passing second, his mind warned him to stop, but it was no use. He was going on pure instinct now. His hands moved from her back to her thighs, pushing up her skirt, finding her skin, tight and hot.

She gasped into his mouth. "Nick, please."

"Show me what you like," he whispered, fueled by her desperate, aching tone. "Show me how to touch you."

She wasted no time in doing as he asked.

Her hands covered his, dragging them up her thighs until he cupped her buttocks firmly. Maggie moaned, thrusting her hips forward sending the lower half of him hard as granite.

That thong. That damn thong.

He groaned, pressing into her, pushing her back against the elevator wall as they shot up to the seventeenth floor. He felt her nipples strain through the thin red fabric of her dress, grazing his chest. She moved against him in a steady rhythm, making him crazy, making his kiss ravenous. And he was. For her.

Then with a chirpy ding, the elevator stopped and the door opened.

They were both breathing heavily, as if they'd just run a marathon in ninety-degree weather. Slowly Nick released her, but his gaze remained fastened on hers, wanting to see that instant of regret he expected to see. But only unsatiated desire shone in those deep-blue eyes.

Maggie was desperate for him, desperate to experience what she'd only dreamed of. For most of her life, she'd been afraid. Of love, lust, being with a man who made her feel. But not tonight.

Tell me how to stop myself from wanting you. When his honest words had hit the heated air around them, it was if the floodgates had opened. She'd tasted what could be, and wanted more.

Her hands plunged into Nick's hair, bringing his head, his mouth back down to hers. He hesitated only a moment, then kissed her with tender hunger, his tongue driving in and out of her mouth as his hands raked up her back. She could stay like that forever, she thought, feeling the roughness of that five-o'clock shadow she found so sexy.

The elevator door closed, then opened again.

"This is our floor, Montana Eyes," he said into her mouth. His tone sounded as desperate as she felt.

"Let's go to our room, then," she whispered, reveling in the intimate sound of his endearment.

He held her slightly away from him, his eyes growing blacker with every heavy breath he took. "If we go into that room, I won't be able to stop this."

She shook her head, her body on fire. "No one's asking you to."

He cursed, then gathered her tighter against him, his mouth taking everything she gave. They stumbled out of the elevator and down the deserted hallway. Maggie clung to him, her heart pounding against her ribs, against him, as she took in every sensation. It was all so new, this feeling of restlessness and urgency. She wanted something, but she wasn't exactly sure what it was or how to get it. But she did know what spurred it on.

Nick.

With one hand around her waist and his mouth occupied, Nick fumbled with the key, then swung the door wide. They were through the living room, into the master bedroom and standing beside the bed in seconds. Nick had torn off his jacket, but Maggie wanted his shirt off, too. Imagining night after night what he felt like, what his skin felt like, only went so far. She wanted the real deal—to feel his chest, his warm skin under her palms. She groped at the tuxedo studs, then got frustrated and ripped the front of his shirt open.

He inhaled sharply, hauled her against the length of him and growled, "Look what you do to me."

Against her belly, she could feel him rock hard and pulsating. She felt no shock, only pride for how she'd affected him. Liquid heat pooled between her legs, and she knew that this need building inside her at a frantic pace had to be satisfied or she'd go insane.

Kissing wasn't enough anymore. How had she ever thought it would be?

Suddenly her gaze caught on his biceps, on the small black tribal symbol tattooed there. She brushed her palm over the intertwined lines, shivers running through her. She'd finally gotten to see it, was her fleeting thought as slowly, gently Nick eased her dress down, his fingers grazing her skin as he went.

That's when he noticed that she wore no bra, only panties.

His gaze raked over her again and again. Mind-blowing desire surged through her blood as he laid her down on the bed, the bed she'd thought about them sharing the night before. He knelt over her, stared at her, watched as her breasts heaved, as her body begged for him to put her out of her misery. The room was dim, lit only by the moon sliding in from the open deck. Dry wind blew the curtains about in an erotic dance.

Nick's ardent gaze found hers as his hand brushed across her silk panties. "You're mine tonight, Maggie."

A shiver passed over her at his words and his touch, possessive and almost carnal. Boldly she grasped both of his hands and guided them to her breasts. Nick sucked in a breath. So did Maggie. It was just a simple touch, but the connection seemed to sear a red-hot bond between them. Then, when his callused palms moved, kneading her flesh, his thumbs coaxing her nipples into taut peaks, analysis gave way to feeling. And when he lowered his head, replacing his hands with his mouth and Maggie nearly came off the bed, feeling gave way to pleasure.

Nick listened to her moans and gave her more of what she liked, flicking her nipple with his tongue, again and again as inside her a fire raged. She pressed her hips up to him, feeling him hard against her. And he met her thrust, teasing her.

But Maggie didn't want to be teased anymore. She wanted Nick with a desperation unlike anything she'd ever felt before. With shaky fingers, she made an unsuccessful attempt to unbutton his pants, pulling at the zipper in frustration. Nick gave a hoarse chuckle, then stood and stripped them off.

He knelt over her, and Maggie gazed at him, at the hard, long length of him. Desire smoldered within her, and she gave in to both, taking him in her hands. He groaned, his eyes closing as she stroked him. Then, like a blind man, his hand found her and traveled downward, over her belly until he slipped beneath the edge of her panties. She gasped as his fingers slid between the wet folds to her core.

"Nick, please," she begged.

"Tell me this is what you want, Maggie," he whispered hoarsely, stroking her lightly. "I need to hear you say that."

"I want it," she assured him. "I want you."

He left her for only a moment, going into the bathroom and returning with a foil packet. He was quick in protecting her, and Maggie was thankful. She needed him now, needed him to quell the deep aching inside her.

Though his breath came ragged just as hers did, he eased off her panties with a gentle tug. When he saw her fully, lying back on the bed, wet and waiting, he wasted no more time. He slid her thighs apart with his knee, rose up and drove into her.

Maggie cried out.

Nick froze.

"Maggie?" The muscles in his arms bunched as he held his position. "You haven't—" His eyes darkened as he looked deep into hers for answers. "You're a virgin?"

She nodded, letting the exquisite pain wash over her as her hands gripped his back. "Yes."

"Why didn't you tell me? I can't—"

"Yes, you can. I want you to. I want it to be you."

The pain faded, and all that sweet urgency returned tenfold. She wrapped her legs around him and pulled him further inside her. Nick groaned, then cursed, his body still as he held his ground. But Maggie was determined. She tilted her hips upward, circling, then thrusting until finally he followed.

Nick moved slowly at first, but soon the tension grew, the need built, and Maggie's thighs quivered and shook. Something was happening, something so foreign and so intense she thought she might die from it. Or live. Really live for the first time.

Instinctively she thrust faster, her mind a blank canvas ready to be painted with brilliant colors. His eyes on her, Nick answered her urgent call, pushed into her hard, demanding, urging her to take her pleasure. And she did. She gasped, her nails digging into his back as pangs of intense pleasure and heat coursed over her in liquid waves. She shot her hips up hard and held there, trying to get him as close as possible. At that, Nick reared back, groaning like a man in the throes of the greatest of agony, the greatest joy. Reaching underneath, gripping her buttocks tightly, he drove into her over and over until he stilled, shuddered, then collapsed beside her.

Morning sun blazed through the bedroom window like a spotlight, examining Nick's actions last night while silently demanding to know what he was going to do about them today. He hugged Maggie infinitely closer, feeling possessive. Her back was to him, giving him a fantastic view of her creamy shoulders and smooth back. She was naked, still asleep, her bottom pressed against his abdomen. Lord, he wanted her again, just as he'd wanted her several times through the night. But he'd abstained—just held her tightly and reveled in the fact that she'd given him a precious gift.

He still couldn't believe she was a virgin at twenty-five. But he loved that she was and found it, he realized, incredibly arousing. Even in the light of day, it amazed him that something so simple had such an effect on him. But it did.

Again his mind drifted back to what had happened in the elevator last night. He was no stranger to desire for a woman. But with Maggie he'd felt like a wild animal, never getting enough, totally out of control—as though her physical being was only the first layer of what he really wanted to get at. And that realization alarmed him. He'd never reacted to a woman like that. And her response to his touch—the unrestrained fire that flooded his senses when his mouth had connected with hers—had acted on him like a drug.

He felt himself grow hard just thinking about it.

Maggie stirred against him, making the situation worse, almost painful.

From the half-open window, an arid breeze fell in step with the shaft of sunlight, forcing him to look at the situation. What would happen now? What did he want to happen? Would she still insist that he date other women in hopes of finding his soul mate? Hell, he wasn't interested in dating anyone—anyone but her, that is.

A new development, not to mention an unsettling one. But it was the truth. And he never denied the truth, even when it was uncomfortable.

But would she really want a guy like him? A guy who got jumpy when he was in one place for longer than six months? A guy who didn't make commitments, came with no promises?

Besides, hadn't she told him that she wasn't even considering dating until after her business was a success, and that she looked at his "match" as part of that success?

Damn, what a mess.

She stirred again, then slowly glanced over her shoulder at him and smiled. An iron fist tightened around his gut as he looked into her sleepy, blue gaze. She was so beautiful. All that rich dark hair tousled about her shoulders.

He brushed aside every concern, nuzzled her neck. "Good morning, Montana Eyes."

"Very good."

Softness radiated from her like the early-morning sunlight hitting his face when he drove through the hills of West Virginia. He pulled her closer. "Last night was wonderful," he whispered in her ear as his hand ran up her belly, over her breasts.

She let out a sigh, still half-asleep.

"I vote for staying here today. What about you?"

She smiled. "I second that."

Staying in this room and forgetting everything past or future. "We'll have to order room service, eat all of our meals in bed."

"Even dinner?"

"Mmm-hmm," he breathed against her shoulder. "But right now I'm hungry for breakfast."

"Me, too." She moved her backside against him. "What are you gonna have?"

On a growl, he flipped her onto her back, grinning down at her. "A little of this." He kissed her mouth softly, then moved to her neck. "Definitely some of this." Down to her stomach, where he nibbled, tickling her, sending her into peals of laughter.

From some indistinct point outside their sensual haze, the phone rang, sharp and shrill. "I forbid you to get that," he said, lazily working his way up to her breasts.

"I have to," she said breathlessly. "What if someone's complained about the noise?"

"Last night?"

"No, silly. This morning."

"Oh, sweetheart, we haven't even begun to make noise."

On a chuckle she turned away from him, her hand darting out to grab the phone. "Hello?"

In one second she vaulted from laughter to pure, tangible fear. "Grandma, slow down— When?" She bolted upright, gripping the receiver, her knuckles white. "I'll be right there."

"What's wrong?" Nick asked.

She jerked out of bed, grabbing the sheet with one hand while she gripped her gold locket with the other.

"Ted was just taken to the hospital."

Seven

———

Life Is Short! Let Maggie Find Someone For You To Share It With.

Maggie splashed some water on her face in the brightly lit hospital bathroom, then took a moment to examine the pale face staring back at her. Puffy eyes filled with worry. Well, she thought with a grim smile at her reflection, everything was just as it should be.

Ted's condition had made everyone anxious, so it was a blessing to find out he was going to be just fine. He had a mild case of heart arrhythmia, and the doctors said that if he felt up to it he could go home as early as tomorrow afternoon. The doctors were very encouraging even as they reminded their patient and his new wife that he needed a good two weeks of rest, some serious relaxation and a lot of love and attention.

Kitty had announced that she would be happy to supply that part of the prescription, then promptly gave Ted a healing kiss on the cheek. She'd stayed by his side in the hospital room, her spirits high, her smile never faltering. But Maggie had seen the fear behind Kitty's eyes and knew what it meant. Kitty didn't want to lose the man she loved. She didn't want to lose another husband.

Maggie dried her hands and left the bathroom. Nick sat in the waiting area, reading a magazine. Her heart soared, then contracted at the sight of him, so calm in the emotion-filled room.

On the way to the hospital, he'd tried to soothe her anxiety, but she hadn't let him—rather she'd pushed him away. She felt wound up, waiting for what could happen next. Her grandma's fears about Ted's condition weighed heavily on her mind, but waking up next to Nick added a further knee-buckling weight.

She didn't want to talk about what had happened—she didn't want to face the fact that she might have made one of the biggest mistakes of her life. Not making love, not giving him her virginity. She would never regret that. But in allowing herself to believe that falling in love with him was possible.

Yes, she knew exactly how Kitty felt, because she felt it, too. Under the guise of short-lived fun, she'd taken the lid off the cookie jar, the jar that held a resolve developed long ago to keep her heart closed, locked away and safe. Sure, the Conner Curse had started out as a childish spook, but it had turned into a defense mechanism—against the risk of abandonment, against the possibility of losing someone she loved.

But ironically, this time, she was more afraid for Nick than she was for herself and her heart.

It didn't matter how ridiculous it sounded, she was afraid that if she pursued anything further with him, something bad could happen to him, just as it had to Ted.

She needed to get back to the business of love. Finding Nick his perfect match. She had to resume their previous arrangement as matchmaker and subject, roommate and landlord to keep him safe from the curse. And hopefully to make her desire for him subside.

Nick looked up as she walked toward him, his eyes filled with concern. "You okay?"

She nodded before she sat down next to him. "Fine."

"Great news, huh? Ted's going to be up and around in a few weeks."

"That's what they say."

"You sound like you don't believe it."

She shrugged. "Life's unpredictable. Especially for the women in my family."

"Is this about that Conner Curse thing?" he asked, tossing his magazine on the low plastic table.

"The Curse is not a joke, Nick."

"Maggie. Ted's okay." He put a hand over hers. "He and Kitty will be—"

She pulled away from him and stood up. Didn't

he understand that his touch made her go soft in all the wrong places? "I didn't thank you for coming with me to the hospital, but I appreciate it and so do Ted and my grandma. Speaking of which, I'm going to go find her."

"She knew you'd say that," he said. "So she asked me to tell you that Ted is resting and she's going to stay with him."

Maggie sighed. "I need to do something."

"Sit down and relax for a minute."

With no other options, she did as he said, but she couldn't relax. God only knew if she could ever relax around him. She wondered if he had this effect on all women, or just her. She wondered so many things about him. His family, his dreams, his favorite song. "Have you ever lost anyone, Nick?"

He took a deep breath and slowly exhaled. "My mother died when I was young."

His eyes were shuttered making it impossible to read what was written there. "I'm so sorry."

"Thanks. So am I."

"And your father…"

"He's healthy, very successful and very stubborn."

"Well, at least now we know you come by it honestly." She chuckled halfheartedly.

He gave her a wry smile. "Actually they were both pretty stubborn."

"I bet your father misses her."

He pressed his lips together, shaking his head. "I wouldn't know. We've never talked about it."

"Maybe you should," she offered.

He nodded. "Maybe. Life's short, right?"

Maggie stilled. Her slogan. Her business slogan, she realized with a flash of understanding, not her life's one.

More than anything, she wanted to move closer to Nick, put her head on his shoulder and let him talk. But she knew that would only serve to suck her in, slowly, like quicksand. "Nick, I called my service and checked my messages."

"And?"

"You had seven requests."

He raised a brow. "Requests for what?"

"A date." She actually felt as if she was choking on the word. "The first two are scheduled for tomorrow. One for breakfast at Hugo's by the Beach and one for dinner at a Latin club downtown. I'm staying here with Kitty and Ted, so I'll call the women and make the arrangements."

He shook his head. "I can't be there."

"Why not?"

"I'm staying with you."

Her heart dropped. "No. You can't. I mean, well, what about your job?"

"My foreman can handle everything for a few days."

Lord, she wanted to fall straight into his arms and say yes, stay, stay with me all day and all night. And then, out of the corner of her eye, she saw her grandma walk out of Ted's room and down the hall to the drinking fountain. Kitty looked exhausted, unsure. Maggie swallowed hard. She wasn't ever going to feel that way.

She glanced over at Nick. He had his cell phone out. He couldn't stay here with her in Las Vegas in the room where they'd made love one more minute much less one more night. If he was close by, she wasn't sure she would be able to keep the commitment she'd made to herself. It was best that he go— back to Santa Flora and on his dates.

"I'm going to call the hotel and book our room for a few more nights," he said, punching in the numbers.

"Thanks, but I'll take care of it."

"It's no problem, Maggie."

She placed a hand over his, stopping him from finishing dialing. "I want you to go home, go on those dates and have a great time."

"No you don't. You want me here."

"Don't tell me what I want, Nick," she said, forcing ice into her tone. Her heart wrenched on each word, but she had to cut him loose to free herself. "We made an agreement, a deal. And my business depends on you following it through to the end."

He stared at her. "And last night?"

She buried everything she wanted to say and, instead, said what she had to say. "Last night was a mistake. It can't happen again. Please understand."

She expected anger, possibly nonchalance, but not sheer, unvarnished disbelief.

"We both know that last night was no mistake. And we both know why you're doing this." His gaze slipped to her locket. "Protection, right?"

She narrowed her eyes at him. "I'm doing this for my business."

"Are you?" He leaned in toward her, his eyes forest green. "You can set me up on dates or push me away all you want, Maggie Conner. But it doesn't change anything. There's something here between you and me, and I promise you, it won't go away until it's run its course." Then he stood. "I'm going to tell Kitty and Ted goodbye now." He turned and walked away, calling over his shoulder, "I'll see you when you get back."

She missed him the minute he was gone. But she knew she'd done the right thing—the only thing she could—to protect the man she was just a breath away from falling in love with.

Wind in his face and gut-twisting speed. That's exactly what he needed. Nick drove his motorcycle down the highway like a bullet with no target in sight.

He'd only been back in town for an hour, but he couldn't bring himself to stay at Maggie's house. He'd stopped in just long enough to drop his bags and jump on his bike. Even without her there, he could feel her presence in that house. Sure, there was no underwear on the shower rod. But he had a real picture of her in his mind now.

A picture of her wearing that wisp of a thong and of him stripping it slowly off her. But the memories didn't stop there. They traveled to more dangerous territory like how, after they'd made love, he just lay there with her, holding her against him, talking about their favorite colors and foods and movies. Before that night with Maggie, he'd never done anything like that in his entire life. But with her it had seemed natural.

Damn, he hated that.

He'd meant what he said to her. He'd fulfill his promise—he'd go out with every Suzie and Sally and Jane. But he'd be coming home to Maggie to finish what they'd started.

He took the next off ramp and pulled onto a winding mountain road. The sun was slowly dipping behind the horizon and the air became chill. The wind wasn't doing a thing to soothe him. It only made him remember how her hair had moved in the breeze when they were dancing.

He'd been her first lover. He couldn't get that fact out of his mind. Along with the possibility that someday, after he'd left town, she would meet someone else. A man who could show her that true love and all that other stuff she believed in for others was also true for her. A man who would stick around and make her see that The Conner Curse was a bunch of bunk. A man who would be the luckiest son of a—

Cursing, he slowed his bike, then stopped. When he removed his helmet and looked up, he cursed again. What was he doing here?

Past a wide expanse of green lawn, rose the three-story, two-winged, Spanish-style villa with five balconies that he'd grown up in. To the left of the three-car garage were acres of fruit trees. He'd climbed each one by the age of eight, helping the pickers to reach the apples and pears. To the house's right was a swimming pool, and behind, a tennis court. He hated tennis—probably because he hated to wear white.

It was a mansion, really, but it hadn't started out that way. When his parents had first bought it, it had been a one-story house on a boatload of land. But his father had built-on a little every few years as his contracting business grew.

It was impressive. And held many good memories to overshadow the bad.

As he stood before it, every fiber of him fought the urge to go into that house. He couldn't help but wonder if his father would once again ask him to drop his little side business to take over the family business.

Nick shook his head. Anthony Kaplan was a good man, decent and hardworking. Nick would give him that. But his questions had always made Nick's life sound worthless, and he wasn't willing to give anyone that kind of power over him.

His new credo stuck like flypaper to his mind.

Life's short.

Just then a gardener spotted him, cocked his head to one side as though he wasn't sure who Nick was. Suddenly he smiled broadly, gave Nick a crisp wave and disappeared behind the house.

Two minutes later Nick's sister bolted out the door.

"Nick, what are you doing here?" Anne asked breathlessly, her long blond hair blowing in the breeze.

"I was in the neighborhood."

She flung her arms around his neck. "Likely

story.'' She stepped back and studied him. ''Well, you've still got the bike, the boots, the jeans—but the hair's gone.''

Nick chuckled. ''I thought you weren't coming home from school until today.''

Anne's eyes flashed. ''How do you know that I didn't?''

To say, ''Because I saw you at the mall when I was clothes shopping with my matchmaker'' didn't sound all that good in his head, so he offered, ''Lucky guess?''

''Try again.''

He rubbed his temples. ''I'm your big brother. You know I have magical powers.''

She rolled her eyes. ''That may have worked on me when I was seven, but not anymore.''

He tried to look pained. ''Are you forgetting the night I made the spirit of Elvis appear for you?''

''That was you in a mask, and by the way it's 'Love Me Tender,' not 'Leave Me Tender.''' She grinned. ''So that was you at the mall?''

He nodded. ''Guilty.''

''Who was the girl?'' she asked.

Nick paused on that one. Who was Maggie? Last night she'd been his lover, this morning… ''She's a friend. My roommate actually.''

Anne nodded sagely, knowing better than to press him. ''Why don't you come in? Dad and I are about to have dinner.''

Nick wanted to. For the first time in a long time, he actually wanted to hang out, talk with Anne about medical school, maybe even talk with his father, try out that tired old cliché—make the peace. But not tonight. He didn't have it to give tonight. He needed to immerse himself in work, get his mind off Maggie for a while.

"I wish I could," he told her, taking in her crest-fallen expression. "I have a ton of building plans to go over before tomorrow. Maybe sometime soon, though."

Anne nodded. "Fine. No problem. Tuesday night will do just as well."

He stared at her wordlessly. Did he even have that night free? How the hell could he explain the flurry of dates he was about to go on? He'd sound like a desperate gigolo. "I don't know, kid. I—"

"I won't take no for an answer, big brother. So give it up." She grinned. "See you at seven. And bring your…what was she again? Oh, yes, your friend and your…"

"Roommate," he supplied with a smirk.

She gave him a short wave and headed back to the house. He wanted to throttle her, but he chuckled instead. Bring Maggie to his family's home. What an idea. Boy, would his father have a field day with that one. Friend? The marrying kind or…?

Nick pulled on his helmet and kicked his bike to a start, revving the engine. Last thing he wanted was for that word to get caught up in the fragile web between Maggie and him.

Nick pulled down the driveway at a reasonable pace, then gunned the thing when he got on the main road. How could his life get any more messy? he thought. And yet something told him that question would probably be answered the minute he went out on his first date.

Maggie pulled up to her house at six o'clock on Monday night. She'd wanted to stay in Las Vegas for as long as her grandma and Ted needed her, but Kitty had insisted that there was nothing for her to do. The hotel was hosting them for the week, so they were going to take some time to recuperate and relax. Kitty had given her a big bear hug and told her to go home to her new business and her nice young man.

Since there was no use in trying to convince her grandma that Nick was not her man and would never be, she'd acquiesced—after making them promise to call in a few days, of course. So she'd headed home, back to Santa Flora, and back to the house she shared with the man she'd shared so much with just a few days ago.

She was exhausted. Lord, it had been impossible to sleep in that hotel bed. Halfway through the night she'd moved to the couch. But he was still there, in her mind, calling her Montana Eyes as he slowly made love to her. All night long she'd still been able to feel his chest against her back.

She exhaled heavily and grabbed her luggage from the cab. They would subside, these feelings. It would just take some time. And for Nick, maybe it would just take one really great date. This morning had been his first, and Maggie had already heard the glowing review from his breakfast partner on her message service. Horrible to admit, but when the woman had said that thirty minutes was far too short a time with Nick, Maggie had felt somewhat relieved. Quick breakfast and out of there.

But tonight was going to be different. At the client's request, Maggie had arranged the whole date from Las Vegas. Dinner and dancing at a great new Latin club in downtown Santa Flora.

The woman had sounded very excited. From seeing his video, she thought Nick was amazing, gorgeous, the perfect guy, and she couldn't wait to meet him. She'd wanted Nick to pick her up, but Maggie was insistent that they meet at the restaurant on their first date.

It was a rule. Something Maggie's Matches insisted upon, she'd told the woman.

Rule, schmule. What a transparent phony she was. She'd never even thought about insisting that a couple meet instead of riding together. It was only going to be a suggestion, a recommendation. But not with Nick's dinner date. Maggie had been firm, and she knew why.

That good-night kiss. His mouth closing in on some other woman's mouth.

And he still had five more dates to go.

Maggie walked to her front door as if she was going to her own funeral. When she reached for the knob, it turned in her hand. Suddenly the door opened and Nick stood there, looking altogether too handsome.

"Hey," he said, his eyes deepening to emeralds as he looked at her. "What are you doing home?"

Her heart stumbled, then fell. She'd thought he'd be gone by now. Scratch that—she'd hoped.

"Kitty has everything under control."

"How's Ted doing?"

Small talk. It was better than the alternatives: her fear, the Conner Curse or her obvious attraction to him. "He's much better. He was up and walking around yesterday. Making jokes." She tried to walk past him. But he didn't move, and being so close to him made her insides jolt around like those Mexican jumping beans she'd spent her entire allowance on when she was ten. She and Kitty had waited all night for them to jump, but they never had.

"So, how'd the date go this morning?" she asked quietly.

"Nice woman, very attractive, but no chemistry." His gaze raked over her. "And that's just something I insist on having."

She swallowed hard at his blatant insinuation, then racked her brain for something innocuous to say. "How's work?"

"Actually, work is great. I'd tell you about it, but—"

"You're on your way out," she finished for him.

He nodded. "Maybe tonight when I get home." It wasn't a question.

Breathless. Again. Damn him. It wasn't fair.

"You'd better go," she said.

His gaze roamed over her. "Yeah, I'd probably better." He moved past her, then stopped and turned back. "So, do I look proper enough for the discriminating Santa Flora tastes?"

He looked good enough to eat. Black jeans, crisp white shirt, tousled hair and heart-stopping eyes. What more could a woman want? But Maggie couldn't say any of the things that were running through her mind, so she opted for a cheery-sounding, "You look very nice, Nick," instead. A little too cheery, she thought. But this was agony, and she'd never really been all that good at pretense.

"Thanks."

"You're wearing cologne."

His grin was slow, almost sinful. "Just trying to please my landlord."

His tone enveloped her, his eyes caressed her. She could so easily fall back into his arms. She wanted to tell him what would really please her at this moment. Him. Staying home with her, sharing a pizza, talking, then making love to her again. Her throat was dry, her skin tight.

She was weak.

He needed to go.

"Well, have a good time." She forced a smile.

"I'll see you later, Maggie."

She turned and walked into the house, then went directly to the window. Was she really sending him off to another woman, she thought as she watched him get on his bike and start it up. Darn right she was.

A dark-yellow tube of fading sunlight beamed down through the trees like an arrow pointing to Nick's right arm, illuminating a shading of what she knew dwelled beneath his shirt. His tattoo.

With her breath caught somewhere between lungs and lips, she wondered if she'd be the only one to see it tonight.

Eight

What a bust.

Nick stood on the busy sidewalk outside the little Spanish restaurant that had played host to one of the worst dates he'd ever had.

From the moment he'd arrived at La Golva an hour and a half ago, he'd known that this setup wasn't going to turn out well. His date had waved him over to the table with the enthusiasm of an airport ground-crew worker, both arms raised above her head, flailing from side to side.

She was pretty, in a funky way. Short brown hair, extreme makeup, wild clothes. One would naturally assume a woman like that would be totally at ease with herself and others.

But that was not the case.

With her eyes wide, she explained over the loud

Latin music that she'd been a bit nervous and had consumed a few margaritas while she was waiting. There were three empty glasses on the table, he noted, aside from the one she was finishing off as she pushed a basket of tortilla chips toward him and demanded that he have some. So "a few" was a pretty relative term.

He ordered some coffee for her and a beer for himself and tried to make conversation. A half hour later she sobered enough to start feeling ill. She apologized profusely. He told her it was no big deal.

In truth, he felt bad for her. If his sister had ever gotten herself into a situation like this, he'd sure hope that her date would look out for her, be a gentleman.

And the gentleman in him told him that this woman shouldn't drive. He wasn't going to take her home on his bike, so it was a cab or several more hours of this pain and suffering. He chose the cab.

He had the cab wait while he saw her to her door, listened as she apologized again, told her he hoped that she'd feel better, then jumped back in the cab and returned to the restaurant to pick up his bike.

Maggie had better be up, he thought, walking toward his bike, which was parked a block from the restaurant. It was only nine o'clock and he had a few choice words for her. Words, he thought with an amused smile, that would hopefully be followed by some kissing and making up.

The ocean looked like liquid coal in the moonlight.

Dressed for a warm summer night, in jeans and a white tank, Maggie sat on the sand, her knees to her chest, and watched the dark waves turn silvery white as they curled, then dropped onto the shore with a crash. An unseasonably warm breeze blew salt air around her, and she breathed it in.

She loved the ocean, loved its dependability. It would always be there. The waves would come in, then go out. With life's constant changes, it was comforting.

Just up the weathered steps in her office, she'd finished off some paperwork, read e-mails and paid bills, almost anything to keep her mind occupied.

But that hadn't lasted very long.

She'd still had to answer the three remaining messages from the women who wanted to meet Nick. She'd called a few and set up dates for Thursday and Friday nights and Saturday afternoon. But after that she'd stopped, her mind consumed with thoughts and questions and images of Nick and his date sitting together in one of the dark corners of La Golva. Were they having a good time? Was he dancing with her the way he'd danced with Maggie in Las Vegas?

"I have a bone to pick with you."

Maggie jumped, sending sand flying through the air all around her. "Nick Kaplan, you do that again and I'll clobber you!"

He snorted and hunkered down next to her. "I'd like to see you try."

"Would you?" she countered, willing her pulse to slow as she fought the urge to pelt him with a fistful of sand.

"Sure." He gave her a lazy grin. "A man is always interested when a woman wants to touch him."

"Even when pain accompanies the touching?" she retorted.

"It wouldn't be pain for long, sweetheart."

His eyes were as dark as the sea and just as dangerous. She almost didn't care that he'd scared her. It was bad for business that he was here with her and not out on his date, but she couldn't stop the relief that swept through her. Then again, she had to ask. "What are you doing here? It's early."

"You set me up with a lush."

"What?" she exclaimed.

"My date was so excited to meet me that she got a little too happy at the happy hour," he said with a heavy dose of annoyance.

"You're kidding," she said, shaking her head in disbelief. Of all the things that could've gone wrong, this was not one she'd imagined.

"No, I'm not kidding." He leaned into her, all the irritation in his voice dripping away like honey from the comb. "So, you're two for two, and I want to know what you're going to do about it."

"Do?" Her voice cracked slightly as his warm breath caressed her neck.

"Considering I didn't pay anything, I know I can't get a refund," he whispered in her ear. "But there's got to be something you can do to compensate me for time misspent."

She inhaled deeply and fought for control over herself. "I just fixed you up on three more dates. How's that?"

He snorted and moved away. "Great. Just great." He shoved a white paper bag at her. "Here."

"What's this?"

"Did you have dinner?"

"No."

"I didn't think so. I went back to the house, and when you weren't there, I knew you'd gone to the office to plan my next date from hell." He gestured toward the bag. "So I stopped and got you a sandwich."

Her lips parted and her heart tugged. She couldn't remember the last time anyone had done anything so spontaneously nice for her. "You didn't have to do this."

He shrugged off her gratitude. "Don't make a big deal of it, Maggie. I thought you'd be hungry, that's all."

"Well, thank you," she said, opening the bag and taking out the enormous sandwich. "There's no way I can eat this by myself. You're going to have to share it with me."

He grinned. "Well, maybe a bite or two. I didn't get to eat much more than a few tortilla chips."

"Here, take half. And don't worry about the other dates, Nick. I'll make sure to set up the next one somewhere safe. Like the zoo or a shopping mall."

"Great," he said with an exaggerated shudder.

She laughed. "Oh, that's right. I forgot about your mall phobia." She knew she should feel bad about his two unsuccessful dating attempts, but strangely, she felt great. They were sitting together at the ocean, under a brilliant moon, sharing a ham and cheese sandwich, and his next date would be at the zoo. Nice, predictable, no good-night kisses, and zero possibility of showing the coveted tattoo. That knowledge filled her with sublime happiness.

They ate in companionable silence. Every now and then when they'd reach for the one napkin they had to share, their hands would brush and their fingers would linger. After a moment she'd pull away and pretend it didn't mean anything. But that didn't stop her from thinking how sweet and thoughtful he was. Or how her life had changed since he'd come. Or how he was going to make some woman very happy someday.

At that thought, her impromptu dinner quickly turned sour in her stomach.

He stood and brushed the sand off his jeans. "You done working for the night?"

"Yep. I think so."

"How about a ride?"

Her eyes snapped to his. "On your motorcycle?"

"I grabbed my spare helmet, so I have an extra."

"I don't think—"

"Good. Don't think."

His offer dangled seductively between them. She'd wanted a ride on his bike ever since that day at the mall. But everything associated with it had one big danger sign attached.

He grabbed her hand and pulled her up. "C'mon, Montana Eyes. I want to take you somewhere."

"Where?"

He put a finger to her lips. "No questions. It's a secret."

He'd never had a woman on his bike before.

It was a sacred thing, his motorcycle. The one

place where he could be alone. He didn't break that
rule for anyone, and he'd been glad when Maggie
had told him that his dates would be meeting him at
their destination.

But he'd made an exception for Maggie. And right
now he didn't want to examine why. He just wanted
to fly with her behind him.

He whipped down a zigzag strip of road, with her
long legs bracketing his thighs and the curve of her
pressing up against his backside. It was enough to
make a man weak, but it only fortified him.

When they'd left her office and started out, she'd
held on to his belt loops gingerly. But as soon as
he'd picked up speed and the salty wind caught them
in its force, she'd wrapped her arms around him and
held on tight.

It was paradise.

He pulled onto a narrow road and stopped at a low,
jagged bluff overlooking the sea. A lonely cloud
passed over the full moon and illuminated the water.
He glanced back at her. She was taking off her helmet, letting her long, dark hair loose. His groin
stirred at the sight, and he turned back to the beach.
The wind had died down and the sky was heavy with
stars.

Maggie stepped off the bike and walked to the
edge of the bluff where a steel gate stopped anyone
from going further, where the beach grass grew high
and thick and melded into the sand.

"This is one beautiful spot," she said, her voice
filled with awe. She pointed toward a large, flat area

where lumber and steel bars lay in neat stacks around a newly poured foundation. "I wonder what this is going to be."

He moved past her and unlocked the gate where the sign declaring Kaplan Construction as the lead contractor on this job hung prominently. "This is the site of the bed and breakfast I'm building," he said, taking her hand and leading her down the grassy rise.

She gasped and squeezed his hand. "Oh, it's a perfect spot. What's it going to look like?"

Nick stopped at the construction trailer and waved a hand in front of the motion detectors to make the floodlights switch on. "Here, I'll show you." He led her down to the beach, grabbed a thin piece of driftwood and broke it in two. With the pointed end of the stick he began to draw a house in a patch of moonlit sand.

"This is the exterior." He glanced over at her and smiled. "I'm no Frank Lloyd Wright, so try and use your imagination."

She laughed quietly. "I'll do my best."

"It'll be a three-story white farmhouse with green trim and a gabled roof," he said as he sketched and pointed. "Here there'll be a wraparound porch with a swing." He drew several small circles in the house. "This will be a chef's kitchen, a large dining room here, a library there, and this will be the billiard room. Very traditional." *Just like you,* he wanted to add.

"When will it be finished?"

"Six months. We're going to be cutting it real

close, but I've hired the best and the quickest. The owners want the place open for the holidays.''

She looked up at him. A cloud passed over her eyes, making them appear sad. ''So they open up shop and you close up shop, right?''

He nodded. ''Soon as the project's done, I'll be on to another job and out of your hair.'' He went to touch that beautiful dark hair but stopped himself. The urge to touch her seemed to be there all the time now. But no matter how much he wanted to, he wasn't making another move without her say so.

This was one helluva romantic spot, though. Not that he'd brought her here with that in mind—which in itself was a little disturbing. No, he'd wanted her to see his work, the thing he loved and was proud of.

''Do you like living that way, Nick?''

The question snagged his attention. He glanced up sharply. ''What way?''

She shrugged. ''Going from place to place. No home.''

''I've got two very comfortable pullout couches in my offices in Seattle and Portland.''

''Yep. Sounds real homey.'' She cocked her head to one side. ''You know what I mean, Nick. No roots, nothing long-term.''

He dragged in a breath. ''You know, when I first started in the contracting business, it was a necessity to travel. I was inexperienced. I needed to go to smaller towns, put in the low bids.'' He crossed his arms over his chest and looked out at the water. ''One time I actually had to put out my own money because my bid was so low. But I had to gain some experience.''

''But now you have a lot of experience and you could stay in one place if you wanted.''

''I guess I could. But I appreciate freedom even more than I appreciate building.'' Over the years the thought of staying put had entered his mind about as often as an eclipse. And even then he'd discarded it. ''I've gotten used to the wandering life. I like it. It would take something pretty unforeseeable for me to set a foundation.''

''Or a pretty someone?'' she offered.

He scrubbed a hand over his face. Didn't she ever let up on that true-love, matchmaking stuff? ''You know, business is important, Maggie. But it's not a life.''

''Sounds like your business is your life, too,'' she said with a trace of defensiveness in her voice. Around them a damp, salty breeze picked up, blowing her hair about her face, and the waves slammed to shore as if echoing her mood.

''I can see how it might look that way,'' he said calmly. ''But I chose this life. Going from place to place, that's freedom to me. It was either that or take over the family business and become my father. And that wasn't the direction I saw my life going in.''

He hadn't wanted to share his past with her, but it was out there now and he couldn't take it back.

''Well, that's what *I'm* doing,'' she said. ''Making a choice, making a life. All I've ever wanted was to feel worth something.''

''But what about a future outside of the business?

Are you ever going to be able to toss that Conner Curse out the window and allow yourself to settle down with a man some day?"

She let out a frustrated sigh. "Why does it matter to you?"

He didn't know why it mattered, it just did, and that fact had his mind twisted into knots.

"What about your future outside business and wandering, Nick? Who's in your future?" She raised a brow at him. "You might want to point that spotlight on your own life and leave mine to me."

Her warning ripped through him like the rocks through the surf. His future, his life—it was going to be more of the same. Devil-may-care suited him, made him happy. But he couldn't imagine Maggie that way—alone, no husband, no kids. He just hoped to hell that he was long gone from Santa Flora before she found such a future.

He muttered an oath. This night was not going as he'd hoped. And it was about to come to an end. "We should go," he said. "It's getting late."

Sweat traveled from temple to jaw and from her jaw to the base of her neck. Maggie whipped off the thin bed sheet and looked at the clock on her nightstand. Twelve thirty-five. Could time go any slower? Could her house be any warmer? It had to be eighty-five eyeball-melting degrees in here. The windows were open as wide as they could go, but the warm air was still, no breeze.

She thought about the location of her fan and grimaced.

Nick's room, closet, top shelf.

Heat assaulted her for a completely different reason.

After her grandma had moved out, Maggie had switched bedrooms. Her grandmother's was twice the size, with a large balcony and built-in bookshelves. Unfortunately, with getting her business up and running and looking for a new roommate, Maggie had left a few things in her old room.

Well, she'd just have to suffer because she certainly wasn't going to knock on her sexy roommate's door at midnight.

She closed her eyes and tried to imagine living in a refrigerator when she heard the shower switch on. Nick. He was probably roasting in his bed, too, and had opted for a cool shower.

At first her mind swirled with images. He was in there, naked, with cool water saturating his tanned skin, droplets beading on his muscled chest and tight stomach.

The fan, Maggie.

Quick as a cat, she bounded out of bed, pulled on her lightest nightie and crept into the hall. The bathroom door was closed, and water continued to run in the shower. She dashed into his room and made a beeline for the closet, avoiding glancing at the bed or anything else. She didn't know why, but she feared the intimacy of it all would slow her down.

She stood on her tiptoes and grabbed the lifesaving fan, but as she brought it down to her chest, she paused. Actually she breathed—breathed deep. The faint, but highly tantalizing scent of his clothes permeated her nostrils. As if she were dreaming, she reached out and touched one of his white work shirts, wondering what it would feel like on her skin and what Nick would think if he saw her wearing it.

On a gasp she dropped the sleeve. The heat was making her think crazy thoughts. She needed to get back to her own room, not to mention reality.

She turned and fled but halfway to the door she ran into a wall of muscle wrapped in a towel.

She groaned inwardly as she forced her gaze up to meet his. And she almost groaned aloud when she did. Amusement and wicked curiosity burned behind those smoky-green eyes.

"I'm hot," she blurted out, then realized the double meaning in her words and wanted to shrink and slither away. Her cheeks on fire, she made a second attempt. "I meant that I *was* hot."

Not much better, Maggie, she thought.

"So you came into my room to cool off?" He raised a brow at her. "Not very flattering."

"Actually this used to be my room." Inane retorts were obviously her strong suit tonight.

Momentarily hypnotized, she watched droplets of water fall from his wet hair onto his shoulder, then move downward over his splendidly muscled chest.

Heat surged into her cheeks. She glanced up sharply, hearing only the tail end of his question.

"...to get that fan?"

She tipped her chin. "Excuse me?"

He chuckled softly. "I asked you if the only reason you came in here was to get that fan."

"Yes, of course," she insisted, wondering if her

tone sounded as defensive as she felt. "What else would I be doing in here?"

He shrugged, but his gaze moved over her, shifting from one hot spot to the next. "Cute pj's. What there is of them, anyway."

She glanced down at her thin cotton baby-doll nightie and wanted to gasp but didn't. You've never been one for panic so don't do it now, she told herself as she fought the urge to run from the room. She lifted her gaze, forced a smile and gave it right back to him. "Nice towel. What there is of it, anyway."

He grinned with sinful intent. "You wanna borrow it so you don't get arrested for indecent exposure?"

"What are you, a cop?" Her voice was like sandpaper, her throat like dust. And her resolve was crumbling. She knew that if he touched her right now—even just a small brush against her—she was done for. Her body craved him like a wolf craves the moon, and her mind wanted to explore every inch of him, know him as intimately as she knew herself.

She cursed the heat, the fan and Nick for getting up to take a shower. "I should go."

He nodded. "Okay."

He stepped aside, and she moved past him at a snail's pace. If he touched her it would be a sign, she thought stupidly, weakly—a sign that Nick could remain untouched by the Conner Curse—a sign that her business would survive even if she gave herself this gift.

One more night with Nick.

"Maggie."

She stopped and looked up at him.

"You're losing something." Yes, my mind, she mused, following his gaze as it slid to her shoulder. The strap of her nightie had slipped down her arm.

She held her breath as he hooked one finger under the strap and dragged it back up her shoulder.

"Now you've done it," she whispered.

He lifted a brow. "Now I've done what?"

"You touched me, Nick."

And then the fan crashed to the floor and her arms went around his neck.

Nine

The animal that dwelled inside of Nick emerged—the animal that only showed its self when Maggie was near. With a guttural sigh he lowered his mouth to hers, then pulled her closer and deepened his kiss. She was right there with him, teetering on the brink of need so raw it had a life of its own as she took his tongue into her mouth.

He was a fool, he thought as he dragged them both away from the door. This thing between them wouldn't run its course and peter out. It was here for the long haul, and he needed to face up to that. Hell, he was crazy about her, and it went way past the physical.

"I want you in my bed," he said, changing the angle of his kiss and the pressure of his mouth. "And you're not going anywhere until I make you as crazy as you make me.''

''Yes.'' She was breathless as her fingers plunged into his hair. ''Yes, Nick.''

It was agony to release her, even a little, but it was the only way. He wanted to see her stretched out on his bed, the way he'd imagined her every night they'd been apart.

Tonight he'd suffered from the heat, too, wrenching the blanket off his bed and leaving just the thin sheet.

With gentle intensity, he set her down on that cool cotton sheet, then stepped back and drank her in for a moment.

She stared up at him, her eyes soft and unbearably seductive, while one corner of her mouth lifted in a provocative smile. She made him happy. That sappy realization was drowned out by the blood in his ears when she stretched her arms out to him, making the light fabric of her nightie inch up over her hips and show him that she wore nothing underneath.

He muttered an oath as he slid into her arms, then murmured, ''Montana Eyes,'' as he eased himself on top of her and took her mouth once again. He nipped at her lips with his teeth, then smiled when she moaned softly and pressed her hips up against him.

He could look into those eyes all night, all day. And Nick reveled in the thought that she was his. Maybe not forever, but tonight she was his.

Her skin felt like hot satin under his palms, and he dragged them slowly up and down her arms as she shivered and made erotic little whimpering sounds.

"I want to feel you, Nick."

"Your skin against mine," he said, and in one frantic move, he ripped off his towel, then grasped the edge of her nightgown, slipping the cotton fabric over her head. He smiled at her, the sudden tenderness in his heart surprising him. "You're so beautiful, Maggie," he said, capturing one creamy shoulder with his mouth, kissing, tasting, feeling more alive than he had in so long. Too long.

He moved to her neck, his tongue pressing into the hollow where her pulse pounded. He swore that the beat thrummed stronger than the last time he had her beneath him. Satisfaction and longing rushed through his blood as he suckled that spot. Maggie pulled in a breath, stirring restlessly beneath him, yet holding his head to her with surprising strength.

"You like this?" he asked, blowing against her damp skin.

"Yes," she uttered, almost winded and frantic. "Don't move. Stay right there."

It took every ounce of control he had to stay where he was when she tasted like heaven and moved against him in a rhythm that was fevered one moment and slow the next.

He moved down her body, his tongue tasting, his hands grazing her skin until he cupped her hips and used his mouth on her.

She gasped. "Nick, I've never—"

"I know, I know. Just let it go, Maggie." He

touched her gently, his fingers stroking the liquid length of her. "Feel how much I want you."

She groaned and he went with her and felt how much she wanted him against his fingers. "Maggie," he breathed, lifting her to his mouth again as his hand moved to her breast.

She gave herself over to him completely then, pressing against him, her knuckles white as she gripped the sheets.

"Nick, please." She looked down at him, and her eyes were the darkest of blue, the deepest shade of passion. "I can't hold on. I want you inside me."

He wanted that, too. He wanted it all.

With one hand he searched the nightstand and grabbed a foil packet. He quickly protected her, then slipped his arms around her and rolled onto his back, taking her with him.

"You're in control now, Maggie." She straddled him and he grinned up at her. "What are you gonna do about it?"

At first she looked adorably unsure, but then she smiled and lifted up over him. Anticipation filled him, saturated the air around them. Lord, he wanted to pull her down, bury himself within her, but he wanted her to feel her own power, he wanted her to guide them into a pleasure new to both of them.

She moved slowly, inching herself down, downward, until he was fully impaled within her. She dragged in a breath, and it was the sweetest sound he'd ever heard. Then she raked her fingernails across his chest and shifted her hips.

He thought he'd lose it right there, but he held on.

She moaned and began to move, riding him. Lifting up, then driving him back into the hot glove of her body.

The light from the hallway behind her made her skin look translucent. She was totally absorbed in the movement, in the feeling. He loved watching her, watching her cheeks turn rosy, her nipples bead and her breath labor and catch.

She was close.

So was he.

Her rhythm changed suddenly and he couldn't hold out. He gripped her hips and guided her up and down at a frantic pace.

She cried out into the humid air, leaning forward and covering his mouth. Their tongues warred for control while he met her in every way, his blood pounding as she tightened around him.

Then she gasped, he growled, and their bodies shattered together.

Lying beside Nick in the semidarkness, her leg draped across his hips, Maggie felt something she'd never felt before.

Possessiveness.

She knew she had no right to feel that way or think of Nick that way, but she didn't care. He had awakened something in her that night in Vegas, something that was buried so deep she'd had no idea it existed. And she wanted those glorious feelings to continue.

It was somewhere around two in the morning and her mind was playing tricks on her. It whispered that Nick was all hers, her lover. It murmured that the curse had lifted and that he would be safe and so would her heart if she asked for what she wanted. And she wasn't going to argue with those deluded, comforting voices right now as she lay naked beside the man she was so desperately in love with.

"We could really use that fan right about now." Nick's amused tone broke through her musings.

"You mean before we both melt into the mattress?"

He pulled her leg closer around him and chuckled. "I can't believe you were going to take the fan out of this room."

"It's my fan, Nick."

He glanced at her, attempting to look crushed. "But I'm your guest."

"You're my roommate," she corrected with a grin.

In a flash he lifted her on top of him again. "Oh, I'm so much more than that."

Feeling him hard beneath her again thrilled her to her toes, but she tried to look unimpressed. "Maybe."

"You better take that back," he warned, his eyes narrowed but full of humor.

She lifted her chin. "Or?"

"Or I'll just have to prey on your weaknesses."

"I'd like to see you try."

"Would you now?" His hands drifted to her waist and squeezed lightly.

She yelped and broke out into a peal of laughter. "Not the tickle torture, please, not the tickle torture."

"Are you going to take back what you said?" he asked his fingers now poised above her kneecaps.

She couldn't stop laughing. "Okay, okay. I take it back. You're more than a roommate. Way more."

His hands stilled and he looked at her closely. She knew what she'd said and how it sounded, but it was the truth and they both knew it.

But all thoughts, all realities were lost as he suddenly gathered her in his arms and kissed her tenderly.

He released her just as easily, but it was too late. She'd felt it—whatever *it* was that had passed between them. Something strange but wonderful, like souls connecting. Her heart had conjured the thought, her mind quickly brushed it aside.

"It's roasting in here," she said, moving off his lap and away from the worrisome thought of tugging off the only thing she wore. Her locket. "I'll plug in the fan."

He grinned like the devil. "I'll watch."

Maggie grinned back as she snatched up the bed sheet and wrapped it around herself. "This isn't a peep show, buddy," she said as she placed the fan on the dresser, accidentally brushing a few things off as she did.

"Shoot." She bent to retrieve them, coming back with a few business cards. Her gaze caught and she held the one on top to the light coming from the hallway. "What's this?"

"Looks like a business card."

She read slowly and aloud. "Anthony Kaplan. 605 Dunhill Road. Santa Flora, CA. And there's a local phone number, too.'' She glanced up at him. ''Who is this?''

''That would be my father.''

''He lives here? You have family here?''

He nodded.

Oh, no, he didn't. ''I can't believe you, Nick Kaplan.'' She put one hand on her hip in mock exasperation. ''You said you had nowhere to stay in this town.''

He leaned back against the headboard, crossed his arms over his chest and sighed, his playful side tucked away for a moment. ''I don't consider my family's home to be a place to stay. My dad and I speak maybe a couple times a year. We don't have much of a relationship.''

Maggie should've felt irritated that he hadn't told her he had family here when they'd discussed housing options that first day in her office. But she couldn't rouse any response but happiness. Never in her life had she felt such blissful happiness. She was beyond glad that he was staying with her, that he'd come with her to Las Vegas and was here now, a naked and very sexy bad boy in her old bed.

But she did feel curious about his past and his obviously bitter feelings about his father.

She sat beside him on the bed and was as tactful as possible. ''If you don't mind my asking, why don't you and your father have a relationship?''

He hesitated, then shrugged. ''Let's just say that I could never please him—never do enough to make him proud. My sister claims that he's changed, hell, *he* claims that he's changed, and maybe I can hear that a little when I talk to him on the phone. But I don't know if I…'' He shook his head. ''I don't want to talk about him right now.'' He took her hand and kissed the palm. ''The truth is, Montana Eyes, I wanted to live here. With you.'' He wiggled his eyebrows. ''Somehow I just knew there'd be some great perks.''

Her heart warmed at his pretty words and his nickname for her. She left the previous subject alone and feigned annoyance. ''You know, I really should punish you for that little fib.''

''Well, who's stopping ya?''

She grinned.

He stretched out on the bed. ''I'll do whatever you want.''

Erotic thoughts filled her mind, but they couldn't override the wants of her heart. ''What I want is two more days with you.'' There she'd said it. All she could say. Because as it was with her mother and grandma, if she dared to utter the words, ''I love you,'' the curse could come on full force.

His brow lifted. ''No dates for forty-eight hours?''

No dates forever, she wanted to say. But this would have to be enough, she thought, even as something inside her warned her that it wouldn't be. Because it hadn't the last time they'd tried to have two days together.

''No dates for forty-eight hours,'' she repeated, moving toward him.

He had her on her back in seconds, his expression untamed. ''I like your punishments.''

She grinned. "So after work tomorrow, you're all mine."

A shadow passed over his eyes. "I have to go to dinner at my family's house. My sister roped me into it." Then, just as quickly it cleared, and he kissed her mouth lightly. "You'll just have to go with me."

After what he'd told her, a peek inside the mind and heart of Nick Kaplan would be very interesting. "I'm game," she said as she ran her hands up his muscled back. "And after dinner?"

He grinned. "We'll come back here and have dessert."

Nick's family's "house" was no house at all. Not by a long shot. It was a sprawling mansion with grounds and a solarium and a full staff.

And an exquisite dining room, Maggie mused, taking mental inventory as she sat down to dinner with Nick and his family.

The oblong space jutted out from the rest of the house, seemingly suspended over the lush backyard, which boasted a verdant forest with stone paths running through it. From her vantage point, it looked like something Hansel and Gretel had skipped through on their way to find the candy house.

Floor-to-ceiling windows made up both walls. And in front of each of those, bronze statues stood on pillars made of white marble. At the very end of the room—which was the closest you could get to the magical woodland outside—was a little stage with a beautiful white grand piano set just off center.

It was a wonderful place. Not the least bit ostentatious, especially for a house of its size. In fact, it was welcoming. Just as the family was, she mused as the housekeeper placed several wonderful smelling dishes on the candlelit table.

"I think Maggie's Matches sounds like the best thing to happen to this sleepy little town in quite some time."

Maggie glanced up and smiled warmly at Nick's father. "Thank you, sir."

"None of that, now." He clucked his tongue. "My father was 'sir.' I'm just Anthony."

It wasn't the first time that Maggie had felt confused since they'd arrived. The way Nick had described his father, she'd expected something along the lines of Ebenezer Scrooge. She could sense some tension between them and Nick was quieter than usual, but it was nowhere close to the animosity she'd expected.

Anthony Kaplan was imposing, she'd give him that, but he was also charming and sweet. And very handsome. He had a full head of gray hair and a clipped beard, dark blue eyes and wide shoulders. At a few inches past six feet, he commanded a room, much the way his son did, with quiet strength.

She'd liked him at once.

And Nick's sister, too. Anne was exactly like Nick had described her on the ride over. Beautiful, clever and very feisty. It had only taken five minutes for Maggie to feel as though she'd made a friend of her. They had laughed uproariously when Anne had filled Maggie in on the details of seeing Nick fall to the ground in the mall's men's store a week earlier.

Maggie hadn't said a word about why she and Nick had really been there. That bit of information would be up to him to share.

But Nick didn't feel capable of sharing much of anything at that moment. He was too busy being completely mystified by the change in his father. His sister had been right. The man seemed almost peaceful now, content. Sure, he and his father had spoken on the phone from time to time, but the changes had seemed small. Nick really hadn't wanted to give the "transformation" much credence, but he sure couldn't ignore it tonight.

He also couldn't ignore the fact that he was having a good time. It seemed that after the initial discomfort he and his father had shared when Nick and Maggie had arrived, they'd both seemed to let go and just relax—entering into some silent pact for tonight.

"Do you think you could find me a good man, Maggie?" Anne asked, taking a sip of wine.

Maggie smiled and nodded. "Absolutely."

"You're too young to date," Nick told his sister, eyes twinkling.

Anne snorted. "I'm twenty-four."

"Yep, way too young." He popped a piece of steak into his mouth for emphasis.

His sister grumbled to her father as the housekeeper poured more wine.

Maggie nudged him with her elbow and whispered, "You do know that I'm twenty-five, right?"

He leaned over and whispered back, "You're an altogether different story."

Nick couldn't help but breathe Maggie in. Her

scent captivated his senses—a combination of roses and vanilla. She also looked stunning in a simple black dress with simple black heels and her hair loose about her shoulders. Simple had never been his thing, but it looked good on her—incredibly sexy on her.

"I've heard some wonderful stories from friends about matchmaking services," Anne remarked. "My roommate went on a couple of really great dates when she signed up at one near our school."

"That's not how Maggie works." Nick shook his head. "She doesn't just find dates for people."

"Oh, really?" Anne said, running a hand through her long, blond hair. "What does she do then, Mr. Smarty-pants?"

He shrugged and said matter-of-factly, "She finds them the love of their life, their soul mate."

Everyone froze, forks at different angles of ascent as they stared at him. How such a defense had come out of his mouth was anybody's guess. Hell, why didn't he just paint a sign that said I'm Really Gone On This Woman and hang it around his neck?

His father's gaze shifted between his son and Maggie. Then he grinned and went back to his garlic mashed potatoes. "Do you think I might still be able to find a soul mate at my age, Maggie?"

"I think you'll just squeak by," she said with a pretty smile. "You just turned thirty, right?"

His father laughed, and Nick shook his head. He sure had to give it to her. She had a way about her and a way with people. She was genuine and natural, charming his father, his sister—not to mention him the first day he'd met her.

"Just bring your ID when you stop by, Anthony," she added.

"I will." He glanced over at Nick. "Maybe when I come down to Maggie's to sign up, you could meet us there. We could all have lunch."

"Things are pretty busy at work," Nick answered automatically.

His father only nodded. "With that bed and breakfast project…right, how's that going?"

"Fine."

Anthony turned to Maggie. "Did you know that my son beat me out of that contract?"

She looked at Nick. "No."

Here it comes, Nick thought. The old "If only he'd come to work for me after college, he could've been doing jobs that size all along and lived in a house as impressive as this one by now."

But his father only smiled. "He's a damned fine contractor." He scooped up some potatoes. "Damned fine."

Nick's eyes narrowed. What was going on? It was like an alternate universe. Praise? From his father? He had absolutely no idea how to respond to it. It was too rare—and entirely too fragile.

"So can you squeeze in a lunch Friday afternoon?" his father asked casually.

Everyone at the table stilled, waiting. Nick felt as though a steamroller was moving across his chest.

Memories of the past shot through his mind like darts. Then that phrase "Life's too short."

He nodded impassively. "All right, Dad."

His father also nodded, said, "Good, good," and continued eating.

Without thinking, Nick reached under the table and took Maggie's hand. She didn't pull away from his grasp, just squeezed as she continued her conversation with Anne about medical school.

Nick didn't exactly know what made him reach for Maggie in such an intimate way. But he didn't examine it. Instead, he reveled in the situation before him. Peace filled this previously disconnected household, and he couldn't help but think that Maggie was partially responsible. For the peace, but what was more important, for the few bricks he and his father had just torn down from the wall that had divided them for so long.

And later, Nick thought, when he and Maggie were alone and the world was still, he'd show her his gratitude.

It was close to midnight when they settled into Nick's bed.

A gentle rain fell outside the open window, cooling the air and scenting the breeze. But inside, beneath his sheets, a fire burned—one he knew would never diminish with Maggie near.

Candles now replaced the hall light, making it easy for him to see Maggie's eyes change color as he pushed into her, driving her over the edge with each stroke.

She wrapped her legs around his waist, pressing him deeper, their bodies moving in time to a silent

song. Pure pleasure rippled over her features as her
soft cries grew louder.

Out of his mind, out of this world, he plunged into
her core. She gasped and tightened around him, her
nails digging into his back as she took him with her,
beyond the moon and into climax.

He stayed inside her and rolled them sideways,
kissing her eyes, her cheeks and finally her mouth,
knowing he'd never felt so exposed in his life. Or so
powerful.

Ten

Would You Recognize The Love Of Your Life If He Walked Up And Introduced Himself? Maggie Would. Let Her Open Your Eyes To The Possibilities.

Maggie gazed across the candlelit table. She knew who the love of her life was. He was sitting here with her on the garden patio of the Sunset Café listening to the soulful sounds of an acoustic guitar player. And, yes—she realized now—she'd recognized him the minute they'd met.

The sweet scent of blueberry pie mingled with the tangy aroma of the nearby ocean. Their dessert sat untouched between them as they watched the entertainment, while, under the table, Nick squeezed her small feet between his larger ones.

It had been a perfect dinner. The food had been

divine and the company extraordinary. All in keeping with the past two days and nights.

Maggie had always thought that sleeping with a man—the actual sleeping part—would be uncomfortable, even disruptive. But she couldn't have been more wrong. With Nick it was comfortable and warm, like napping under a tree on that perfect summer day when it's neither too hot nor too cool.

And to wake up with his arms wrapped around her, feeling his strength—what she wouldn't give for a lifetime of mornings like that.

Her mind swam with possibilities she'd always been too afraid to consider. Every second she spent with him she felt her fear lessening and those irrational beliefs from the past floating away. Could it happen? Could she and Nick do the impossible: foil the curse?

Even if it were possible, she could never say to him, "I'm in love with you, Nick. Stop running and stay here with me. Let's share our days and our nights together and build a family of our own."

He'd never given her any indication that he wanted more, that he wanted a relationship. What he *had* told her was that he was leaving after his job ended.

"Where are you, Montana Eyes?"

Maggie's head came up with a snap. "I'm here," she said with a guileless smile. Oh, Lord, did he always have to look so good? So dark and dangerous? He wore a smoky-gray shirt, black pants and a killer smile. His thick, brown hair was tousled, his eyes a deep green and he hadn't shaved since the morning.

Longing surged through her heart. Longing and a

profound sadness. Beginning tomorrow he was going to stay at his father's house. He had a week full of dates scheduled—dates that couldn't be canceled now—and he didn't want to stay at Maggie's while that was going on.

Ironically, this time he'd given her no arguments about finishing out his commitment to her, no complaints. And, because she was slowly going nuts, her mind had already begun conjuring up all sorts of horrible scenarios: he was looking forward to the dates; he was anxious to meet more women; he'd had enough of her and was ready to move on to the next conquest.

"Maggie? Are you all right?"

Her wandering mind cleared and focused on the man who sat across the table from her, the man who was filling her nights with unimaginable pleasure and her days with unending worry. "Fine. Just a little full."

"You can't leave here without at least one bite of this pie. It's their specialty." He scooped up his fork, cut a sliver of blueberry and crust and vanilla ice cream and held it out to her. "You don't have to do a thing. This mouthful of decadence is coming straight to you."

She laughed as he held the fork to her lips. "You sound like a TV commercial."

He grinned, moving his fork toward her slowly. "The rich, plump blueberries burst on your tongue in a symphony of sweetness and juicy delight."

"I think you missed your calling, Nick Kaplan," she said, then devoured the bite.

"Hidden talents should remain hidden," he said.

"I don't agree. I say put it all out there on the table and see what happens."

"Is that a fact?" He studied her with a twinkle in his eye. "Listen, I happen to know what amazing talents you have, Maggie, but what I'd really be interested in is what you *do* have hidden. Like something about a locket, maybe?"

As if guided by some cosmic force, her hand went to the gold oval at her throat. "I thought you would've forgotten about that."

"Not a chance." He took a sip of coffee. "Or were you just talking about me putting it all out on the table a second ago?"

Of course she was. Didn't he understand women at all? "It's just something to remember my father by, okay?" Odd, that didn't feel as painful to say as she'd always thought it might.

"I thought you'd never met your dad."

"I didn't...I haven't."

"C'mon, Maggie," he said, taking her hand and kissing her palm. "Talk to me. You know plenty about my family. Give a little here, maybe it'll feel good."

She wanted to do what she usually did at a moment like this—laugh casually and divert the conversation. But she didn't see the point this time. Nick was stubborn when he wanted something, and she wasn't in the mood to fight him. It was just history. Besides, he'd shared his family—and his family secrets—with her.

"My mother met him at the beach during a summer break from college. He was a professional surfer, and all the women were just crazy for him. Tall, tan, handsome and all that.'' She felt herself smile. ''He only had eyes for my mother, though. The way my mom told it to me, it was all very Frankie Avalon and Annette Funicello at first. Bonfires and picnics and long days in the sun. But one night at the beach, on the sand, they…'' Maggie heard her mother's voice in her own as she told the story and her heart ached. ''A few weeks later she told him she was pregnant. And he told her he was leaving the next day for Hawaii.''

Nick's eyes were filled with understanding, though he couldn't possibly. ''He gave her that locket before he left?''

''No,'' she said softly. ''He sort of left what's inside it.''

He didn't press her on that, and she was grateful. ''You know, it's entirely possible that you could have a completely different life from your mom's.''

''I guess anything's possible, right?''

''Right.'' He kissed her palm again and said, ''What do you say to a late movie?''

A movie was the last thing she needed. She needed him close, naked and beside her, making her forget the past and future for a few hours. ''What do you say to having them wrap up this delicious slice of berry heaven and taking it home.''

''Dessert in bed again?''

She grinned.

''I love the way you think, Montana Eyes.''

And I love you, Nick Kaplan.

* * *

Power dating. It was the only way to describe what he'd been doing over the past week. Five women in seven days. It had to be some kind of record, he thought as he pulled into the parking lot of the Santa Flora newspaper, the *Seaside Press.*

The ladies he'd been matched with had all been pleasant and attractive. One of them was actually up for the interior decorating job for the bed and breakfast. So, needless to say, he'd had no trouble making conversation.

There'd been no upsets like that date at the Latin club. However, like those first two dates, he just wasn't interested in anything more than conversation. He'd been a gentleman—charming and friendly—but when it came to the possibility of good-night interplay, his mind would fill with images of Maggie. So he'd tactfully excuse himself, and the night would end.

Never in his life had a woman captured his mind and his heart the way Maggie had. Every night he'd fly down the ocean highway on his bike, breaking the speed limit two times over. He'd needed it to clear his head and calm his body.

It had worked for a short time. But Maggie was a powerful force. Lying in bed at night, all he wanted was for her to be next to him. He missed their banter, their disagreements, that flash of smile when she was embarrassed or surprised.

Her phone calls to him about the dates were brief and businesslike, although he could feel that she missed him, too. Admittedly, they both had to fulfill the bargain that had started this whole thing before they could move on. But the more he was away from her, staying at his father's and dreaming of her at night, the more he thought he'd like to give a relationship with her a go. He couldn't offer anything permanent, but he knew he definitely wanted to see her more and often.

He chuckled as he walked through the big double doors of the *Press*. This wasn't like him at all. He'd never been a one-woman man, hadn't wanted to be, for that matter. The idea of actually trying it had crept up on him slowly, so slowly he couldn't seem to stop it.

But somehow he knew he had to give it a shot.

And tomorrow night after his last date, he was going home to her, he was going to take her in his arms and tell her that he wanted a break from dating. Dating anyone but her, that is, he mused as he stepped up to the reception desk and gave his name.

He was about to tilt his sword to his own aversion to relationships in the only way he knew how—and as an added bonus, he was giving the Santa Flora newspaper a great story and giving Maggie some good publicity.

It would be his gift to her to let her know that after all his griping and protests about matchmaking services, he believed in her. She'd have to wait a few days to see the story, though, until the article about her grand opening on Saturday night ran in the business section. But it would be worth it.

Her query that night on the beach brushed through

his mind. "You could stay in one place if you wanted," she'd said.

He wanted, he thought as he waited for the reporter to come and get him. For now he definitely wanted.

The next day Maggie woke up early and retrieved her messages from her voice mail. After a slew of sales calls and advertising pitches, she learned that Nick's last date had canceled. The poor young lady had the flu and could barely lift her head off the pillow.

For exactly one minute Maggie tried to feel disappointed—after all, finding Nick as many dates as possible had been her goal.

But it was no use.

Happiness and relief filled every inch of her as she jumped out of bed, tossed on her robe and trotted down the stairs with a twenty-four-karat smile.

Maybe she should call Nick right now, she thought, tell him to get home—or better yet, she could go on the date tonight in her sick client's place. A surprise. Oh, what would he think if she walked into the restaurant in that red Vegas dress and sat down beside him?

What *would* he think, she wondered, coming face-to-face with herself in the hallway mirror. Sure, they'd had a few nights of fun together, but what was their future? Lord, did they even have one? From day one, Nick had warned her that he didn't believe in love, relationships, soul mates or permanency of any kind. And in less than six months he was leaving Santa Flora.

Was she up for having a six-month affair? Could her heart let him go when the time was up?

Her gaze slid downward in the mirror. The gold locket at the base of her throat winked tauntingly, reminding her not to forget its power—asking her if she was really willing to risk a few amazing months for a lifetime of sorrow, not to mention potential harm to the man she loved.

Turning away from the mirror, she tried to clear her mind, but the effort wouldn't take right away. For most of her life she'd given in to the overwhelming strength of her fear. Was she going to do it again? she wondered as she went outside and grabbed the newspaper.

She went into the kitchen and poured herself a cup of coffee. Maybe she'd immerse herself in work today, try to put all questions, all worries, aside for a few hours. Her grand opening was tomorrow night, and though she had everything pretty much under control, there were still a few things to be done.

Expelling an apprehensive breath, Maggie sat down at the kitchen table with her coffee and flipped through the pages of newsprint. She'd put a full-page ad in today's paper to invite all of Santa Flora to the grand opening. Hopefully, they'd made no mistakes and it was as eye-catching as she'd planned. Tossing a couple of lumps of sugar into her cup with one hand, she thumbed through the pages with the other.

Suddenly she froze.

Opposite the ad was an interview. An interview

with *Nick*. The headline screamed, Maggie's Made Me A Match!

With wide, disbelieving eyes, she scanned the contents of the article. "I was a skeptic, but the service really works.... If you're looking for your soul mate, go to Maggie's Matches.... Maggie found me the woman of my dreams."

Her mouth felt like cotton, her heart thundered like the hoofbeats of a wild horse. Nick had found the woman of his dreams? How was it possible? Why hadn't he told her? Of course, they hadn't spoken much, and when they had he'd acted a little distant. But she'd just chalked that up to annoyance for having to follow through on dates he'd been forced to go on.

It had only been a week, she thought dimly, her throat tight as a steel trap. Was it love at first sight? Lord, she'd always known it could happen. In the beginning it's what she'd hoped for. But now...

She threw the paper down, her coffee cup skittered sideways as she put her head in her trembling hands. How could she have been such an idiot? How could she have let herself believe that it was possible to challenge the curse? And win?

And most foolish of all, how could she think that Nick Kaplan might ever be able to care about her the way she did him?

She was the matchmaker. She'd promised him she'd find him the love of his life—and she'd done it. Yippee, she thought, tears welling in her eyes. Hallelujah.

She came to her feet slowly. Hot tears rolled down

her cheeks and she swiped them away, her gaze shooting to the phone. All that needed to be said could be said over the phone, right? She didn't have to see him in person, look in his eyes, searching pathetically for the possibility that it was all a mistake—that he wanted her the same way she wanted him.

All those questions went unanswered. She knew she was going to that restaurant tonight. Just as she knew that today she was going to have to prepare herself for one of the finest acting jobs of her life.

Because tonight she had to pretend that Nick Kaplan meant nothing to her at all, except a really great, really heartbreaking headline.

"Can I get you a drink, sir?"

Nick glanced up at the waitress and smiled. "I'll take a beer."

He was in a really good mood. The B and B was going up fast and the crew was doing a fine job. He and his father had a—he hated to use the word—*date* to play golf next week. He didn't know squat about the game, but what the hell, it was good to finally have a friend in the man.

Nick had told his father about his plans with Maggie, his plans to stay in town. And Anthony Kaplan hadn't said one word about taking over his company when he gave Nick a hug and said, "Welcome home, son."

Who would have thought it? His life was coming together. But, more important, tonight was his last date, the fulfillment of his promise to Maggie. She had completion on her little experiment, however misguided, and now he could have her.

He glanced at his watch. Seven-thirty. Where was his date, anyway? he wondered, moving his gaze to the front door.

A few couples were strolling in, but no single lady. Maybe he was going to be stood up, he thought with a slow grin. Then his gaze caught. He squinted. Was that Maggie? His pulse raced. It sure was, and in a tight white T-shirt and a long pink skirt, she looked good enough to eat.

He stood up as she walked toward him.

"Hello, Nick."

"Maggie, what are you doing here? Is everything all right?"

"Your date couldn't make it."

"Thank God, because I'm through with dating." Yep, he thought with a smile. This day couldn't get any better. "Why don't you sit down? I'll get you something to drink."

"No, thanks. I can't stay."

Why wasn't she looking at him? Her voice was so cool and distant. In fact, her expression seemed completely detached. They hadn't seen each other in a week. Maybe she wasn't quite sure what to say. He opted for humor. "So this officially ends the dating season, then?"

She nodded stiffly. "That's part of why I came."

"Really?" That sounded promising.

"Listen, Nick. I wanted to thank you for holding up your end of the bargain." She lifted her chin. "I think your experience is going to be exactly what

I need to get men to come and sign up for my service.''

''I'm glad.'' Nick's smile began to fade. She was acting like a damn iceberg. ''So what's next?'' he asked, hoping for some clues to her abrupt attitude change.

''Just taking advantage of all that free press for my business, and then—'' she took a quick breath and shrugged lightly ''—on to my next project.''

He frowned. Her next project? Okay, so maybe they started out that way—working on a project together. But that had all changed, hadn't it?

''I've already had about twenty calls from men eager to sign up,'' she continued. ''The grand opening should be a total success.''

He cursed silently. Success? Why the hell had he even done this whole project if men were signing up, anyway—and before he officially became her poster child? What a sucker. He'd been sitting here, mooning over her and making plans and she was back to business and thinking about her *next project?*

He looked across the table at her. Had he really misjudged her that much? Thought she wanted him, felt something for him? Or was he just one helluva delusional jackass? Because it sounded as if she was saying that he'd served his purpose in her life and now she was finished with him.

''So, that's it, then?'' he asked, giving her an inch, hoping that would bring her back—back to the way she was when he'd held her in his arms just a week ago.

She nodded tightly, looking anywhere but at him.

"Pretty much." Then she cast a glance toward the exit. "Oh, one more thing. Do you mind coming by the shop tomorrow night?" she asked, pressing her lips together. "Talk to a few reporters?"

Hell, that was it, the nail in the coffin. It really had been "just business." A phrase he knew all too well and should've stuck by the moment he'd laid eyes on her.

"Sure, no problem," he answered, gripping his beer bottle so tightly he wouldn't have been surprised if it shattered. For ten years he'd been the one who could see an affair as an affair and nothing more; he'd been the one who danced the fine line, trying not to inflict more pain than necessary. How the hell could he have switched roles and not even known it?

Well, today was payback time, apparently.

He could hardly wait until this business was finished. Until he could move forward again. No looking back, no regrets.

"I appreciate your doing this." Her eyes were shuttered. "So, I'll see you tomorrow?"

"Yeah. See you, Maggie."

He watched her walk out of the restaurant, feeling as though she'd taken his heart with her. But it was only temporary, he told himself, downing his beer. He'd recover. Out on the road. It was the best place—and the only place he truly belonged.

He held up his empty beer bottle and nodded at the bartender.

Out on the road.

Only this time he'd save himself some trouble and stay far, far away from that damn Montana sky.

Eleven

—

There's Someone Out There For Everyone. Your Perfect Match Awaits. Maggie Brings Hearts Together.

"Where should I put these, Maggie?"

Standing behind the reception desk, Maggie stared at the three banners in Kitty's hands, banners she'd ordered a week ago. When she'd felt truly inspired.

It was already 10:00 a.m. and she'd had about fifty RSVPs for the opening tonight. In nine hours Maggie's Matches would be packed with Santa Flora singles ready and hoping to make a love connection.

And her dream would become a reality.

She should have felt on top of the world, but instead she felt like hiding under the covers with her good buddies Ben and Jerry and crying into her chunky monkey.

But what good would that do?

Everything, her pride, her happiness—not to mention her savings—was riding on her business being a success, and she couldn't let her feelings for Nick stop her from accomplishing her goals.

Lord, but she missed him—his touch and his voice. The hardest part was that she couldn't find it in her heart to be angry with him. They'd both been willing participants. No one had uttered words like *commitment* or *love* or *relationship,* even if one of them had felt eager to hear them. If anyone was at fault for her broken heart, she was, and she had to acknowledge that. All along she'd been the driving force behind Nick finding that someone special.

And he had.

And *she* had to be happy for him. But that didn't stop her from loving him, and she doubted it ever would.

Last night when she'd gotten home from the restaurant, she'd picked up the phone to call him. But she'd stopped herself. What could she say that wouldn't put him in the awkward position of telling her he didn't feel the same?

It was her first broken heart. First and last. From now on, she would put everything she had inside her into her work. Over time she knew she would start to erase him from her mind and from her soul. The best she could do now was never mention she loved him to anyone, then maybe the curse would leave him alone and let him enjoy his life with whoever it was that he'd fallen in love with.

"Maggie?"

She glanced up sharply. "I'm sorry, Grandma." She brushed all thoughts of him from her mind and touched the banners that her grandma held out for inspection. "Why don't we put one above the front desk, one outside and one…"

"Around Nick's chest?" Kitty chided.

"In the video lounge," Maggie said weakly. Well, that forgetting-Nick concept had lasted, oh, about ten seconds. She saw him in her mind, bare-chested and grinning with sex appeal, her banner stretching from muscled shoulder to tapered waist. She exhaled heavily, turned away from her grandma and began fumbling through a bag of decorations in search of God knew what.

"You should have told him how you feel, Maggie."

I couldn't. "I'll get over it."

"It's not that easy. Love's not like a faucet to be turned on and off."

"Well, I'm certainly going to try." And if turning off the faucet didn't work, she thought, pulling out a bag of heart-shaped balloons, she'd have the water disconnected altogether.

Kitty grabbed a few balloons. "He obviously did that interview for you."

For me, just not about me. "And I appreciate it. I really do. It's bringing in the guys, just like I wanted." She shook her head. "But why couldn't he have told me first? Why didn't he tell me that he'd found the woman of his dreams?"

"I don't know, sweetie." Kitty tried to blow some air into the small balloon, but nothing happened, and she gave up and pitched it back into the bag. "I'll tell you one thing, though. That man loves you. I've been a matchmaker for fifty years. I know the signs."

Maggie's heart squeezed at the thought. She couldn't believe that Nick loved her. It was like the day that Paula Jenson had told her that Santa Claus didn't exist. For hours after school that day she'd cried against Kitty's chest while her grandma had wrapped her arms around a seven-year-old and very disillusioned Maggie. But when the tears had dried, Kitty had practically scolded her for believing such utter nonsense. "I've seen him many times, even spoken to him. And he wouldn't appreciate you spreading a rumor like that any further."

To this day Maggie still liked to believe that Santa was out there.

Kitty had been most convincing. And nothing much had changed, Maggie thought as a little voice inside her whispered that her grandma did have the experience—that she saw things that other people didn't.

Lord, more than anything Maggie wanted to slide down into the warm, comforting fantasy her grandma had painted. But this time she couldn't deny her reality.

She had lost Nick.

Oh, who was she kidding? she thought, grabbing the balloons and heading for her office. She'd never really had him to begin with.

Nick went through his mental Rolodex in search of a contractor who had the skills and the resources to finish the bed and breakfast for him, because after tonight he needed to get out of this town and away from Maggie Conner.

Well, first he'd probably want to get drunk, then he'd get out of town.

He hunkered down on the steps of the construction trailer and stared out at the water slapping its white foamy beard against the shore.

He didn't like to admit it even to himself, but he'd missed living here, near the ocean. In his younger days, he'd have been out there body surfing, enjoying the moment, being a carefree kid. It was the one place where he didn't have to think.

Today the air was warm, even though thin clouds passed over the summer sun from time to time. But what the hell, he thought, reaching down to unlace his work boots. Maybe a dip in the surf was exactly what he needed. He had a lot to forget. Like a sexy raven-haired goddess with eyes that would haunt him forever.

"I thought I'd find you here."

Nick jerked his gaze up and saw his father walking toward him.

"I used to come out to my sites when times got tough. Sometimes it felt like the only place I could think."

"Home away from home?" Nick cringed at the resentful tone in his own voice. Time heals all wounds, huh? he asked himself. He sure as hell hoped so.

His father sat down next to him on the steps. He was silent for a moment, then he took a deep breath.

"I'm sorry about not being around for you and your sister when you were kids, Nick. I was trying to build a business and forgot about my family. I had nothing growing up, less than nothing, and I wanted better for my children."

As luck would have it, Nick now understood that kind of drive. To prove your worth to others and to yourself.

His father turned to look at him. "I can't go back and change what was, but I can apologize for how hard I tried to turn you into..."

"You?"

"Well, yeah." He chuckled. "And I'm real glad that I couldn't. You're one helluva man, Nick. I'm proud of you."

It didn't make Nick see hearts and flowers, but it was something. In fact, it was the something he'd wanted to hear for years. And it sounded good.

"So if you'll let me, I'd like to start being that father right now. You look like you could use one."

Nick stood up. "Well, actually, I could use your help."

"Name it."

"I'm looking to leave town early. Could you put one of your managers on this job and take it over?"

"You have another job to go to?"

"No."

His father slowly came to his feet. Nick noticed for the first time that they were almost exactly the same height, same build. But his father's eyes held a steady pain that he never wanted to inherit.

The man put a hand on Nick's shoulder. "I could,

but I think you're looking for a different kind of help, Nick.''

"What does that mean?"

"You don't want to leave here."

His father had no idea what was going on. How could he? "You're wrong."

"Did you tell her that you love her?"

"Hell, no. I—" He stopped, knifed a hand through his hair. How in the hell did his father know what had happened between him and Maggie? He'd never given him details of their relationship. And, anyway, it didn't matter, because nothing had actually happened between them.

"I don't love her," he said finally. Damn, he couldn't even have a conversation without it turning to Maggie. She'd invaded his life, his thoughts, his dreams. He woke up reaching for her and went to bed longing for her.

What was he supposed to do? She didn't give a damn for him. She'd made that clear. And he wasn't going to run after her no matter what he felt. That highway was closed for repairs.

"I don't believe you, son," his father said. "I think you're crazy about her."

"No. I'm just plain crazy," he stated through gritted teeth. "For the last time, Dad, Maggie's out of my life."

His father took a rolled-up newspaper from his jacket pocket. "Then what's this all about?"

On a curse Nick snatched the paper. Grumbling about meddlesome parents, Nick glanced down. There was Maggie's advertisement. So she'd run an ad for her business. Why wouldn't she? It was obviously all she cared about.

"What's what all about, Dad?"

"Stop being a stubborn jackass and take a closer look," he said as he walked off toward the B and B's foundation. "I'll be over there looking at your handiwork if you need me."

Nick looked down at the newspaper again and his gaze caught on the headline on the page that faced Maggie's ad:

Maggie Makes a Match!

He stared at the headline. His article wasn't supposed to run until tomorrow. Why would they run it today when—

His gaze shifted to the date of publication.

Friday. Yesterday.

A stream of curses fell from his lips. Those idiots at the *Press* had run his article two days early. He shook his head, trying to get the fog to clear. Had Maggie seen it? Of course she had—his article was positioned right across from the ad she'd placed.

His mind reeled, then filtered back to last night and the way she'd looked at him. Oh, yeah, she'd read this thing. There was no doubt in his mind. So that meant that she'd probably thought he'd found the woman of his dreams…and she'd no idea who he'd been talking about.

Something close to a growl erupted from his throat. No wonder she'd acted like the North Pole in winter.

He scrubbed a hand over his face. He was a jackass, so quick to assume that she didn't want him.

Too afraid of being caged to open his eyes and see that Maggie Conner was the one person on earth who had set him free.

He'd been ready to take off, leave his newly rediscovered family and the biggest job his company had had so far because of that fear. This misery he'd felt every night since he'd left her was his own.

Now it was time to make a choice. Did he want to be an angry drifter forever, or go find the woman he loved and tell her—

He froze. The realization moved over him like the clouds moved across the sun, illuminating and darkening, darkening and illuminating again.

It wasn't possible. Not a guy like him. A dry laugh escaped his throat. But it was possible. He loved Maggie. Loved everything about her. Her drive, her blind faith and the way she threw herself fully into everything she did.

The way she believed in him and his heart.

He shook his head. It might already be too late, he knew. He may have already lost her, but he'd be damned if he'd give up that easily.

He walked over to his father who was staring out over the ocean from the bluff where the B and B would stand. The waves roared so loudly Nick had to put his hand on his father's shoulder to get his attention. When his father turned around, Nick said simply, "I love her."

"I know, son. You look just like I did the day I married your mother."

In a thousand years, Nick never thought he'd be hearing something so personal from this man—hell,

Nick never imagined confiding that he'd actually fallen in love. But life had a sense of humor and a forgiving heart.

Nick exhaled heavily, a smile coming to his lips. "You want to go to a party tonight?"

"Only if you're going to come home with that girl on your arm."

Nick chuckled. "If she'll have me, Dad. If she'll have me."

Maggie opened her doors at seven o'clock. And by seven-thirty the grand opening of Maggie's Matches was an official success.

And it wasn't just Maggie's opinion, either. She heard the buzz all around her—the excitement from all the singles who seemed confident that Maggie could help them meet their match. Their voices filled the air like the strains of an orchestra preparing to perform. A few reporters milled about, eating, drinking—some even making love connections of their own.

The atmosphere was certainly conducive to romance. The lights in the reception area were dimmed, and a hundred heart-shaped votive candles flickered from every surface like so many stars in the sky. The ocean sent a soft breeze through the open doors and windows, batting the balloons and streamers about. The caterer stood over the elegant spread of bruschetta, ground lamb wrapped in phyllo, assorted cheeses and fruit and the most delectable-looking miniature éclairs, while a man dressed in black tie served champagne in sparkling crystal.

It was perfect.

The only thing missing was Nick.

For the hundredth time that day, she wondered if he would really come tonight. And if he did, would he bring the woman from the article? She inhaled deeply, trying to steady her breathing. Seeing him with another woman, his arm linked with hers, her gaze sweeping his face—every now and again they'd kiss and Maggie would die a little more inside.

No one would suspect, though. So far she'd kept a brave face, smiling, thrilled with her opening and the thirty-five new clients she had signed up so far.

She glanced around the room, spotting a few of the ladies she'd set him up with, their sights set on new prey.

Then her heart fell into her heels.

Nick stood by the door, talking to a woman. But this woman gave Maggie no palpitations. It was her grandma who stood there, talking animatedly to Ted, Nick and his father. Easy confidence emanated from Nick, as if he belonged here and defied anyone to tell him differently.

She allowed her gaze to move over him, though her misery grew with every inch she perused. But she couldn't help it; she still felt as though he belonged to her. Because she knew him inside and out. Or she'd thought she had.

His hair had grown some since he'd had it cut, and it now licked the collar of his dark-green dress shirt. His eyes were darker than normal, but his smile was easy. Lord, suit and tie had never looked so good on any bad boy. Her fingers itched just thinking about loosening that tie, unbuttoning those buttons...

She closed her eyes and turned around. They didn't have to talk tonight or even see each other. Presumably, after he moved the rest of his things into his father's house, she'd hand him a check and never have to see him again.

She needed a minute to compose herself, try to quell the ache in her heart. She was already halfway out the back door to do just that when she heard a familiar baritone say, "Excuse me, ladies and gentlemen."

Her feet felt as if they were stuck in quicksand, and her lungs refused to pull in any air. Silence quickly enveloped the room like an imposing fog.

"My name is Nick Kaplan, and I'm here to give a testimonial."

Slowly Maggie turned, horror filling her at the prospect of listening to him tell the world about the wonderful woman who had stolen his heart—the woman she'd introduced him to.

His gaze scanned the room. Then he spotted her, and he smiled, slow and sinful. "I'm a cynic," he told the crowd as a flashbulb went off. "I've always believed that love was the worst of all four-letter words. Actually I believed that love was for fools. So when Maggie told me—actually she guaranteed me—that she could find me the love of my life, I think I laughed." He raised a brow at her. "I laughed, right, Maggie?"

Everyone turned to look at her. She nodded

bleakly. What had started out as a successful evening was quickly turning into a nightmare.

"But she was right," he continued. "Maggie Conner found me the woman who has changed me forever...just plain ruined me for other women." He chuckled and looked around. "And that's saying something."

The room erupted in laughter, while inside Maggie her heart shrank.

Nick sobered, his eyes—those magnetic green pools—searched her own. "I told the reporter from the *Press* that Maggie had found me that woman, my soul mate. But I didn't give him her name."

A hush seeped through the crowd. Maggie felt as though a sponge was stuck in her throat, slowly expanding with each new revelation. She didn't want to hear any more. She didn't want to hear the name of the woman who'd stolen the heart of the man she loved.

She wanted to run, but she couldn't seem to move. His gaze held her where she was.

He smiled at her, a very tender smile. "Her name is Maggie Conner."

Another flashbulb went off, a distinct gasp sounded somewhere in the room as the crowd murmured amongst themselves.

Maggie stilled, totally submerged in disbelief. She'd heard him wrong. Maggie Conner was the woman who brought us together, that's what he'd said. But no, around her, people stared, whispered the very words she would swear she'd only imagined him saying.

"Now, guys," he said, his face growing more serious as he looked around the room. "I took the cream of the crop, so she's off-limits." He grinned. "But if I can find that perfect woman, I guarantee that you can, too. Good luck."

Nick felt about as confident as a toddler trying to stand for the first time as he walked down the steps and through the crowd. But he didn't give a damn. If all went as planned, in about five seconds he'd be holding the woman he loved in his arms.

Around him guests chattered quietly, trying to appear as if they weren't watching to see what happened next. But he could feel their eyes on him.

He came to stand before her. She looked shaken, and he had no idea what that meant.

"Hi," he said.

"Hi," she said softly.

"Can we talk?"

She nodded, her eyes wide and luminous.

"Outside?"

She nodded again.

He didn't wait for the shock to wear off. He took her hand and led her outside. And they kept on walking, down the steps, to the moonlit beach, until they couldn't hear the crowd, the music—until they couldn't hear anything but the familiar sound of the waves rolling up onto the sand.

"I don't understand, Nick. That article…"

Her voice was broken, confused and unsure, and all he wanted to do was hold her and tell her what was in his heart, but after what he'd unwittingly put her through, she deserved an explanation. "Maggie, that article was supposed to have come out tomorrow. It was supposed to have been a love letter. From me to you.''

She gasped, tears springing to her eyes. ''But, I thought...''

''I know, I know,'' he said gathering her in his arms. ''You thought that I'd fallen in love with one of those women you set me up with.''

''But you didn't.'' It wasn't a question, rather a confirmation.

The anxiety in her voice tore at him, but he couldn't stop from smiling. She was here, in his arms. ''No, I didn't.'' He held her away from him slightly, lifting her chin to his gaze. ''I love *you*, Montana Eyes.''

Maggie stood there, staring up at him on legs as weak as water. If this was a dream, she prayed, never let me wake up. ''Say it again, Nick.'' She was tempting the Fates, but she needed to hear it again, over and over, until it made sense in her bruised and muddled mind.

He kissed her softly. ''I love you. Everything about you. You are my perfect match, my soul mate.'' His gaze grew serious. ''Let me be that for you.''

Inside her, it was like Las Vegas all over again. Bells ringing, shouts of joy, cries of happiness—and the remnants of a fear still deeply imbedded. ''I love you, too, Nick. So much. And I want everything you have to give.'' She looked away. She had everything, right here, but somehow she just couldn't take it. ''But I'm still afraid.''

"Of what?"

"The Conner Curse." The ocean breeze blew her hair about her face. "I know it sounds silly and stupid, but, Nick, I'm really afraid I'll lose you."

"Sweetheart, I promise you, I'm not going anywhere," he said, though his eyes glowed with understanding. "But just in case, I may have the perfect antidote." He grinned, his arms tightening around her. "How about changing your name to Kaplan?"

"What?"

He released her then, pulled a small gold box from his jacket pocket and handed it to her. Her heart soared like the seagulls overhead. He loved her and he wanted her.

With shaky fingers, she opened the box. A beautiful sapphire ring surrounded by tiny diamonds winked back at her. "It was my mother's. My father gave it to me this afternoon. He thought I might need it tonight."

Tears filled her eyes. How could such an ill-fated girl end up so lucky?

As the waves lifted and crashed, Nick lowered to one knee. "Marry me, Maggie. Be my wife."

"Oh, yes," she said softly, smiling, then breaking out into joyful laughter. "Yes, Nick. Yes." Suddenly she sobered as she remembered the tie to the past that would always bind her unless she gave it up for good.

"There's just one thing."

His eyes darkened with worry as he slowly got to his feet.

With heartfelt determination, she lifted the neck-

lace and locket over her head. "I have to do something first." The cool gold felt heavy now. She
opened the oval and tossed the heavy grains of sand
it contained into the air. "This sand was from the
spot where my mom and dad said goodbye. I thought
it would always remind me to keep my heart closed
and safe." But it didn't have that power, Maggie
thought as she bent and took another bit of sand from
the ground between them.

With steady fingers this time, she dropped the
creamy-colored grains into the locket, snapped it
closed, then looked up at Nick. "Now it will be a
reminder of you. The man who taught me to live and
love and trust again."

He had her in his arms in seconds, covering her
mouth with his own. He kissed her deep and long as
the wind picked up around them and the waves in
turn answered. When he finally pulled his lips from
hers, her knees no longer felt like rubber. She felt
strong, her heart completely filled.

Under the glowing moon, she tipped her chin up
and looked into his eyes. "I love you like crazy, Nick
Kaplan. And I can't wait to be your wife."

He scooped her up in his arms and smiled. "Let's
not wait, then," he said. "How does next Saturday
sound?"

She laughed. Lord, he could always make her
laugh. Her arms went around his neck as she lowered
her lashes and played coy for a moment. "I need
some time to get a dress and some flowers, maybe
take a little time to get to know your family."

He held her against his chest, against his heart. "They're your family now, Maggie."

A true and honest warmth spread through her soul. She had everything she could ever want in this man. A real success story. And she was forever grateful.

"Let's go, sweetheart." He turned and started up the beach. "We have some of that family waiting impatiently to hear if you said yes or not."

"That's a lot of steps." She cast a look over her shoulder to the steps that led to her shop. "Do you want to put me down?"

He grinned at her. "Never. Besides I need the practice." Then he winked. "You know, for the threshold?"

They moved away from the darkness of the beach and toward the light of their future. With a contented sigh Maggie let her head fall against his shoulder. "Who'd have believed it? From my first customer to my husband in one fell swoop."

He kissed the top of her head. "And I assure you, Montana Eyes, I'm the most satisfied customer you are ever going to have."

* * * * *

And don't miss Laura Wright's
next Silhouette Desire

BABY & THE BEAST

In December 2002

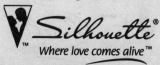

If you enjoyed what you just read,
then we've got an offer you can't resist!

Take 2 bestselling love stories FREE!

Plus get a FREE surprise gift!

Clip this page and mail it to Silhouette Reader Service™

IN U.S.A.	IN CANADA
3010 Walden Ave.	P.O. Box 609
P.O. Box 1867	Fort Erie, Ontario
Buffalo, N.Y. 14240-1867	L2A 5X3

YES! Please send me 2 free Silhouette Desire® novels and my free surprise gift. After receiving them, if I don't wish to receive anymore, I can return the shipping statement marked cancel. If I don't cancel, I will receive 6 brand-new novels every month, before they're available in stores! In the U.S.A., bill me at the bargain price of $3.57 plus 25¢ shipping and handling per book and applicable sales tax, if any*. In Canada, bill me at the bargain price of $4.24 plus 25¢ shipping and handling per book and applicable taxes**. That's the complete price and a savings of at least 10% off the cover prices—what a great deal! I understand that accepting the 2 free books and gift places me under no obligation ever to buy any books. I can always return a shipment and cancel at any time. Even if I never buy another book from Silhouette, the 2 free books and gift are mine to keep forever.

225 SDN DNUP
326 SDN DNUQ

Name	(PLEASE PRINT)	
Address	Apt.#	
City	State/Prov.	Zip/Postal Code

* Terms and prices subject to change without notice. Sales tax applicable in N.Y.
** Canadian residents will be charged applicable provincial taxes and GST.
  All orders subject to approval. Offer limited to one per household and not valid to
  current Silhouette Desire® subscribers.
  ® are registered trademarks of Harlequin Books S.A., used under license.

DES02   ©1998 Harlequin Enterprises Limited

SINTMAG

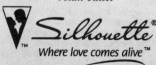

COMING NEXT MONTH

#1471 All in the Game—Barbara Boswell
She had come to an island paradise as a reality game show contestant. But
Shannen Cullen hadn't expected to come face-to-face with the man who had
broken her heart nine years ago. Sexy Tynan Howe was back, and wreaking
havoc on Shannen's emotions. She was falling in love with him all over again,
but could she trust him?

#1472 Expecting…and in Danger—Eileen Wilks
Dynasties: The Connellys
They had been lovers—for a night. Now, five months later, Charlotte Masters
was pregnant and on the run. When Rafe Connelly found her, he proposed a
marriage of convenience. Because she was wary of her handsome protector, she
refused, yet nothing could have prepared her for the healing—and
passion—that awaited her in his embrace….

#1473 Delaney's Desert Sheikh—Brenda Jackson
Sheikh Jamal Ari Yasir had come to his friend's cabin for some rest
and relaxation. But his plans were turned upside down when sassy
Delaney Westmoreland arrived. Though they agreed to stay out of each
other's way, they eventually gave in to their undeniable attraction. Yet
when his vacation ended, would Jamal do his duty and marry the woman his
family had chosen, or would he follow his heart?

#1474 Taming the Prince—Elizabeth Bevarly
Crown and Glory
Shane Cordello was more than just strong muscles and a handsome face—
he was also next in line for the throne of Penwyck. Then, as Shane and his
escort, Sara Wallington, were en route to Penwyck, their plane was hijacked.
And as the danger surrounding them escalated, so did their passion. But upon
their return, could Sara transform the royal prince into a willing husband?

#1475 A Lawman in Her Stocking—Kathie DeNosky
Vowing not to have her heart broken again, Brenna Montgomery moved to
Texas to start a new life—only to find her vow tested when her matchmaking
grandmother introduced her to gorgeous Dylan Chandler. The handsome
sheriff made her ache with desire, but could he also heal her battered heart?

#1476 Do You Take This Enemy?—Sara Orwig
Stallion Pass
When widowed rancher Gabriel Brant disregarded a generations-old family
feud and proposed a marriage of convenience to beautiful—and pregnant—
Ashley Ryder, he did so because it was an arrangement that would benefit
both of them. But his lovely bride stirred his senses, and he soon found
himself falling under her spell. Somehow Gabe had to show Ashley that he
could love, honor and cherish her—forever!

SDCNM1002